M

W

*

A HOUSE OF GENTLEFOLK

*

*

The Works of Ivan Turgenev

NOVELS

Rudin
A House of Gentlefolk
On the Eve
Fathers and Children
Smoke
Virgin Soil (2 vols.)
A Sportsman's Sketches (2 vols.)

STORIES

Dream Tales and Prose Poems
The Torrents of Spring
A Lear of the Steppes
The Diary of a Superfluous Man
A Desperate Character
The Jew

*

IVAN TURGENEV

*

A HOUSE OF
GENTLEFOLK

*

Translated from the Russian by
CONSTANCE GARNETT

HEINEMANN · LONDON

William Heinemann Ltd
LONDON MELBOURNE TORONTO
JOHANNESBURG AUCKLAND

434 79901 7

First published 1897
Reprinted 1905
Limited Edition 1906
Large Type Fine-Paper Edition 1907
Reprinted 1914, 1915, 1917, 1919
Library Edition 1920
Reissued 1970

Printed in Great Britain by
WESTERN PRINTING SERVICES LTD,
BRISTOL

THE NAMES OF THE CHARACTERS
IN THE BOOK

MÁRYA DMÍTRIEVNA KALÍTIN.
MÁRFA TIMOF-YÉVNA PÉSTOV.
SERGÉI PETRÓVITCH GEDEÓNOVSKY.
FÉDOR (*pr. Fyódor*) IVÁNITCH LAVRÉTSKY
ELISAVÉTA MIHÁLOVNA (LISA).
LÉNOTCHKA.
SHÚROTCHKA.
NASTÁSYA KÁRPOVNA.
VLADÍMIR NIKOLÁITCH PÁNSHIN.
CHRISTOPHER FÉDORITCH LEMM.
PIÓTR ANDRÉITCH LAVRÉTSKY.
ANNA PÁVLOVNA.
IVÁN PETRÓVITCH.
GLAFÍRA PETRÓVNA.
MALÁNYA SERGYÉVNA.
MIHALÉVITCH.
PÁVEL PETRÓVITCH KOROBÝIN.
KALLIÓPA KÁRLOVNA.
VARVÁRA PÁVLOVNA.
ANTÓN.
APRÁXYA.
AGÁFYA VLÁSYEVNA.

In transcribing the Russian names into English—
　　a has the sound of *a* in *father*.
　　e 　　,,　　,, *a* in *pane*.
　　i 　　,,　　,, *ee*.
　　u 　　,,　　,, *oo*.
　　y is always consonantal except when it is
　　　　the last letter of the word.
　　g is always hard.

A bright spring day was fading into evening. High overhead in the clear heavens small rosy clouds seemed hardly to
move across the sky but to be sinking into its depths of blue.

In a handsome house in one of the outlying streets of the
government town of O—— (it was in the year 1842) two
women were sitting at an open window; one was about fifty,
the other an old lady of seventy.

The name of the former was Marya Dmitrievna Kalitin.
Her husband, a shrewd determined man of obstinate bilious
temperament, had been dead for ten years. He had been a
provincial public prosecutor, noted in his own day as a successful man of business. He had received a fair education and had
been to the university; but having been born in narrow circumstances he realised early in life the necessity of pushing
his own way in the world and making money. It had been a
love-match on Marya Dmitrievna's side. He was not bad-
looking, was clever and could be very agreeable when he
chose. Marya Dmitrievna Pestov—that was her maiden name
—had lost her parents in childhood. She spent some years in
a boarding-school in Moscow, and after leaving school, lived
on the family estate of Pokrovskoe, about forty miles from
O——, with her aunt and her elder brother. This brother
soon after obtained a post in Petersburg, and made them a
scanty allowance. He treated his aunt and sister very shabbily
till his sudden death cut short his career. Marya Dmitrievna
inherited Pokrovskoe, but she did not live there long. Two
years after her marriage with Kalitin, who succeeded in winning her heart in a few days, Pokrovskoe was exchanged for
another estate, which yielded a much larger income, but was
utterly unattractive and had no house. At the same time
Kalitin took a house in the town of O——, in which he and
his wife took up their permanent abode. There was a large
garden round the house, which on one side looked out upon
the open country away from the town.

'And so,' decided Kalitin, who had a great distaste for the
quiet of country life, 'there would be no need for them to be
dragging themselves off into the country'. In her heart Marya

Dmitrievna more than once regretted her pretty Pokrovskoe, with its babbling brook, its wide meadows, and green copses; but she never opposed her husband in anything and had the greatest veneration for his wisdom and knowledge of the world. When after fifteen years of married life he died leaving her with a son and two daughters, Marya Dmitrievna had grown so accustomed to her house and to town life that she had no inclination to leave O——.

In her youth Marya Dmitrievna had always been spoken of as a pretty blonde; and at fifty her features had not lost all charm, though they were somewhat coarser and less delicate in outline. She was more sentimental than kind-hearted; and even at her mature age, she retained the manners of the boarding-school. She was self-indulgent and easily put out, even moved to tears when she was crossed in any of her habits. She was, however, very sweet and agreeable when all her wishes were carried out and none opposed her. Her house was among the pleasantest in the town. She had a considerable fortune, not so much from her own property as from her husband's savings. Her two daughters were living with her; her son was being educated in one of the best government schools in Petersburg.

The old lady sitting with Marya Dmitrievna at the window was her father's sister, the same aunt with whom she had once spent some solitary years in Pokrovskoe. Her name was Marfa Timofyevna Pestov. She had a reputation for eccentricity as she was a woman of an independent character, told everyone the truth to his face, and even in the most straitened circumstances behaved just as if she had a fortune at her disposal. She could not endure Kalitin, and directly her niece married him, she removed to her little property, where for ten whole years she lived in a smoky peasants' hut. Marya Dmitrievna was a little afraid of her. A little sharp-nosed woman with black hair and keen eyes even in her old age, Marfa Timofyevna walked briskly, held herself upright and spoke quickly and clearly in a sharp ringing voice. She always wore a white cap and a white dressing-jacket.

'What's the matter with you?' she asked Marya Dmitrievna suddenly. 'What are you sighing about, pray?'

'Nothing,' answered the latter. 'What exquisite clouds!'

'You feel sorry for them, eh?'

Marya Dmitrievna made no reply.

'Why is it Gedeonovsky does not come?' observed Marfa Timofyevna, moving her knitting needles quickly. (She was knitting a large woollen scarf.) 'He would have sighed with you—or at least he'd have had some fib to tell you.'

'How hard you always are on him! Sergei Petrovitch is a worthy man.'

'Worthy!' repeated the old lady scornfully.

'And how devoted he was to my poor husband!' observed Marya Dmitrievna; 'even now he cannot speak of him without emotion.'

'And no wonder! it was he who picked him out of the gutter,' muttered Marfa Timofyevna, and her knitting needles moved faster than ever.

'He looks so meek and mild,' she began again, 'with his grey head, but he no sooner opens his mouth than out comes a lie or a slander. And to think of his having the rank of a councillor! To be sure, though, he's only a village priest's son.'

'Everyone has faults, auntie; that is his weak point, no doubt. Sergei Petrovitch has had no education: of course he does not speak French, still, say what you like, he is an agreeable man.'

'Yes, he is always ready to kiss your hands. He does not speak French—that's no great loss. I am not over strong in the French lingo myself. It would be better if he could not speak at all; he would not tell lies then. But here he is—speak of the devil,' added Marfa Timofyevna looking into the street. 'Here comes your agreeable man striding along. What a lanky creature he is, just like a stork!'

Marya Dmitrievna began to arrange her curls. Marfa Timofyevna looked at her ironically.

'What's that, not a grey hair surely? You must speak to your Palashka, what can she be thinking about?'

'Really, auntie, you are always so . . .' muttered Marya Dmitrievna in a tone of vexation, drumming on the arm of her chair with her finger-tips.

'Sergei Petrovitch Gedeonovsky!' was announced in a shrill piping voice, by a rosy-cheeked little page who made his appearance at the door.

[3]

✳ 2 ✳

A tall man entered, wearing a tidy overcoat, rather short trousers, grey doeskin gloves, and two neckties—a black one outside, and a white one below it. There was an air of decorum and propriety in everything about him, from his prosperous countenance and smoothly-brushed hair, to his low-heeled, noiseless boots. He bowed first to the lady of the house, then to Marfa Timofyevna, and slowly drawing off his gloves, he advanced to take Marya Dmitrievna's hand. After kissing it respectfully twice he seated himself with deliberation in an arm-chair, and rubbing the very tips of his fingers together, he observed with a smile—

'And is Elisaveta Mihalovna quite well?'

'Yes,' replied Marya Dmitrievna, 'she's in the garden.'

'And Elena Mihalovna?'

'Lenotchka's in the garden too. Is there no news?'

'There is indeed!' replied the visitor, slowly blinking his eyes and pursing up his mouth. 'Hm! . . . yes, indeed, there is a piece of news, and very surprising news too. Lavretsky—Fedor Ivanitch is here.'

'Fedya?' cried Marfa Timofyevna. 'Are you sure you are not romancing, my good man?'

'No, indeed, I saw him myself.'

'Well, that does not prove it.'

'Fedor Ivanitch looked much more robust,' continued Gedeonovsky, affecting not to have heard Marfa Timofyevna's last remark. 'Fedor Ivanitch is broader and has quite a colour.'

'He looked more robust,' said Marya Dmitrievna, dwelling on each syllable. 'I should have thought he had little enough to make him look robust.'

'Yes, indeed,' observed Gedeonovsky; 'any other man in Fedor Ivanitch's position would have hesitated to appear in society.'

'Why so, pray?' interposed Marfa Timofyevna. 'What nonsense are you talking! The man's come back to his home—where would you have him go? And has he been to blame, I should like to know!'

[4]

'The husband is always to blame, madam, I venture to assure you, when a wife misconducts herself.'

'You say that, my good sir, because you have never been married yourself.' Gedeonovsky listened with a forced smile.

'If I may be so inquisitive,' he asked, after a short pause, 'for whom is that pretty scarf intended?'

Marfa Timofyevna gave him a sharp look.

'It's intended,' she replied, 'for a man who does not talk scandal, nor play the hypocrite, nor tell lies, if there's such a man to be found in the world. I know Fedya well; he was only to blame in being too good to his wife. To be sure, he married for love, and no good ever comes of those love-matches,' added the old lady, with a sidelong glance at Marya Dmitrievna, as she got up from her place. 'And now, my good sir, you may attack any one you like, even me if you choose; I'm going, I will not hinder you.' And Marfa Timofyevna walked away.

'That's always how she is,' said Marya Dmitrievna, following her aunt with her eyes.

'We must remember your aunt's age . . . there's no help for it,' replied Gedeonovsky. 'She spoke of a man not playing the hypocrite. But who is not hypocritical nowadays? It's the age we live in. One of my friends, a most worthy man, and, I assure you, a man of no mean position, used to say, that nowadays the very hens can't pick up a grain of corn without hypocrisy—they always approach it from one side. But when I look at you, dear lady—your character is so truly angelic; let me kiss your little snow-white hand!'

Marya Dmitrievna with a faint smile held out her plump hand to him with the little finger held apart from the rest. He pressed his lips to it, and she drew her chair nearer to him, and bending a little towards him, asked in an undertone—

'So you saw him? Was he really—all right—quite well and cheerful?'

'Yes, he was well and cheerful,' replied Gedeonovsky in a whisper.

'You haven't heard where his wife is now?'

'She was lately in Paris; now, they say, she has gone away to Italy.'

'It is terrible, indeed—Fedya's position; I wonder how he

can bear it. Everyone, of course, has trouble; but he, one may say, has been made the talk of all Europe.'

Gedeonovsky sighed.

'Yes, indeed, yes, indeed. They do say, you know that she associates with artists and musicians, and as the saying is, with strange creatures of all kinds. She has lost all sense of shame completely.'

'I am deeply, deeply grieved,' said Marya Dmitrievna. 'On account of our relationship; you know, Sergei Petrovitch, he's my cousin many times removed.'

'Of course, of course. Don't I know everything that concerns your family? I should hope so, indeed.'

'Will he come to see us—what do you think?'

'One would suppose so; though, they say, he is intending to go home to his country place.'

Marya Dmitrievna lifted her eyes to heaven.

'Ah, Sergei Petrovitch, Sergei Petrovitch, when I think how careful we women ought to be in our conduct!'

'There are women and women, Marya Dmitrievna. There are unhappily such . . . of flighty character . . . and at a certain age too, and then they are not brought up in good principles.' (Sergei Petrovitch drew a blue-checked handkerchief out of his pocket and began to unfold it.) 'There are such women, no doubt.' (Sergei Petrovitch applied a corner of the handkerchief first to one and then to the other eye.) 'But speaking generally, if one takes into consideration, I mean . . . the dust in the town is really extraordinary to-day,' he wound up.

'*Maman, maman,*' cried a pretty little girl of eleven running into the room, 'Vladimir Nikolaitch is coming on horseback!'

Marya Dmitrievna got up; Sergei Petrovitch also rose and made a bow. 'Our humble respects to Elena Mihalovna,' he said, and turning aside into a corner for good manners, he began blowing his long straight nose.

'What a splendid horse he has!' continued the little girl. 'He was at the gate just now, he told Lisa and me he would dismount at the steps.'

The sound of hoofs was heard; and a graceful man, riding a beautiful bay horse, was seen in the street, and stopped at the open window.

＊ 3 ＊

'How do you do, Marya Dmitrievna?' cried the young man in a pleasant, ringing voice. 'How do you like my new purchase?'

Marya Dmitrievna went up to the window.

'How do you do, *Woldemar*! Ah, what a splendid horse! Where did you buy it?'

'I bought it from the army contractor. . . . He made me pay for it too, the brigand!'

'What's its name?'

'Orlando. . . . But it's a stupid name; I want to change it . . . *Eh bien, eh bien, mon garçon*. . . . What a restless beast it is!'

The horse snorted, pawed the ground, and shook the foam off the bit.

'Lenotchka, stroke him, don't be afraid.'

The little girl stretched her hand out of the window, but Orlando suddenly reared and started. The rider with perfect self-possession gave it a cut with the whip across the neck, and keeping a tight grip with his legs forced it in spite of its opposition, to stand still again at the window.

'*Prenez garde, prenez garde*,' Marya Dmitrievna kept repeating.

'Lenotchka, pat him,' said the young man, 'I won't let him be perverse.'

The little girl again stretched out her hand and timidly patted the quivering nostrils of the horse, who kept fidgeting and champing the bit.

'Bravo!' cried Marya Dmitrievna, 'but now get off and come in to us.'

The rider adroitly turned his horse, gave him a touch of the spur, and galloping down the street soon reached the courtyard. A minute later he ran into the drawing-room by the door from the hall, flourishing his whip; at the same moment there appeared in the other doorway a tall, slender dark-haired girl of nineteen, Marya Dmitrievna's eldest daughter, Lisa.

＊ 4 ＊

The name of the young man whom we have just introduced to the reader was Vladimir Nikolaitch Panshin. He served in Petersburg on special commissions in the department of internal affairs. He had come to the town of O—— to carry out some temporary government commissions, and was in attendance on the Governor-General Zonnenberg, to whom he happened to be distantly related. Panshin's father, a retired cavalry officer and a notorious gambler, was a man with insinuating eyes, a battered countenance, and a nervous twitch about the mouth. He spent his whole life hanging about the aristocratic world; frequented the English clubs of both capitals, and had the reputation of a smart, not very trustworthy, but jolly-natured fellow. In spite of his smartness, he was almost always on the brink of ruin, and the property he left his son was small and heavily encumbered. To make up for that, however, he did exert himself, after his own fashion, over his son's education. Vladimir Nikolaitch spoke French very well, English well, and German badly; that is the proper thing: fashionable people would be ashamed to speak German well; but to utter an occasional—generally a humorous—phrase in German is quite correct, *c'est même très chic*, as the Parisians of Petersburg express themselves. By the time he was fifteen, Vladimir knew how to enter any drawing-room without embarrassment, how to move about in it gracefully and to leave it at the appropriate moment. Panshin's father gained many connections for his son. He never lost an opportunity, while shuffling the cards between two rubbers, or playing a successful trump, of dropping a hint about his Volodka to any personage of importance who was a devotee of cards. And Vladimir, too, during his residence at the university, which he left without a very brilliant degree, formed an acquaintance with several young men of quality, and gained an entry into the best houses. He was received cordially everywhere: he was very good-looking, easy in his manners, amusing, always in good health, and ready for everything; respectful, when he ought to be; insolent, when he dared to be; excellent company, *un charmant garçon*. The promised land lay before him. Panshin quickly learnt the secret of getting on in the world; he knew how to yield with genuine respect to its decrees; he knew how to take up trifles with half ironical seriousness, and to appear to regard everything serious as trifling; he was a capital dancer; and dressed in the English style. In a short time he gained the reputation of being one of the smartest and most attractive young men in Petersburg. Panshin was indeed very smart, not less so than his father; but he was also very talented. He did everything well; he sang charmingly, sketched with spirit, wrote verses, and was a very fair actor. He was only twenty-eight, and he was already a *Kammer-yunker*, and had a very good position. Panshin had complete confidence in himself, in his own intelligence, and his own penetration; he made his way with light-hearted assurance, everything went smoothly with him. He was used to being liked by everyone, old and young, and imagined that he understood people, especially women: he certainly under-stood their ordinary weaknesses. As a man of artistic lean-ings, he was conscious of a capacity for passion, for being carried away, even for enthusiasm, and, consequently, he permitted himself various irregularities; he was dissipated, associated with persons not belonging to good society, and, in general, conducted himself in a free and easy manner; but at heart he was cold and false, and at the moment of the most boisterous revelry his sharp brown eye was always alert, taking everything in. This bold, independent young man could never forget himself and be completely carried away. To his credit it must be said, that he never boasted of his conquests. He had found his way into Marya Dmitrievna's house immediately he arrived in O——, and was soon per-fectly at home there. Marya Dmitrievna absolutely adored him. Panshin exchanged cordial greetings with everyone in the room; he shook hands with Marya Dmitrievna and Lisa-veta Mihalovna, clapped Gedeonovsky lightly on the shoulder, and turning round on his heels, put his hand on Lenotchka's head and kissed her on the forehead.

'Aren't you afraid to ride such a vicious horse?' Marya Dmitrievna questioned him.

'I assure you he's very quiet, but I will tell you what I am afraid of: I'm afraid to play preference with Sergei Petrovitch; yesterday he cleaned me out of everything at Madame Byelenitsin's.'

Gedeonovsky gave a thin, sympathetic little laugh; he was anxious to be in favour with the brilliant young official from Petersburg—the governor's favourite. In conversation with Marya Dmitrievna, he often alluded to Panshin's remarkable abilities. Indeed, he used to argue how can one help admiring him? The young man is making his way in the highest spheres, he is an exemplary official, and not a bit of pride about him. And, in fact, even in Petersburg Panshin was reckoned a capable official; he got through a great deal of work; he spoke of it lightly as befits a man of the world who does not attach any special importance to his labours, but he never hesitated in carrying out orders. The authorities like such subordinates; he himself had no doubt, that if he chose, he could be a minister in time.

'You are pleased to say that I cleaned you out,' replied Gedeonovsky; 'but who was it won twelve roubles of me last week and more?' . . .

'You're a malicious fellow,' Panshin interrupted, with genial but somewhat contemptuous carelessness, and, paying him no further attention, he went up to Lisa.

'I cannot get the overture of Oberon here,' he began. 'Madame Byelenitsin was boasting when she said she had all the classical music: in reality she has nothing but polkas and waltzes, but I have already written to Moscow, and within a week you will have the overture. By the way,' he went on, 'I wrote a new song yesterday, the words too are mine, would you care for me to sing it? I don't know how far it is successful. Madame Byelenitsin thought it very pretty, but her words mean nothing. I should like to know what you think of it. But I think, though, that had better be later on.'

'Why later on?' interposed Marya Dmitrievna, 'why not now?'

'I obey,' replied Panshin, with a peculiar bright and sweet smile, which came and went suddenly on his face. He drew up a chair with his knee, sat down to the piano, and striking a few chords began to sing, articulating the words clearly, the following song—

Above the earth the moon floats high
    Amid pale clouds;
Its magic light in that far sky
    Yet stirs the floods.

My heart has found a moon to rule
    Its stormy sea;
To joy and sorrow it is moved
    Only by thee.

My soul is full of love's cruel smart,
    And longing vain;
But thou art calm, as that cold moon,
    That knows not pain.

The second couplet was sung by Panshin with special power and expression, the sound of waves was heard in the stormy accompaniment. After the words 'and longing vain', he sighed softly, dropped his eyes and let his voice gradually die away, *morendo*. When he had finished, Lisa praised the motive, Marya Dmitrievna cried, 'Charming!' but Gedeonovsky went so far as to exclaim, 'Ravishing poetry, and music equally ravishing!' Lenotchka looked with childish reverence at the singer. In short, everyone present was delighted with the young dilettante's composition; but at the door leading into the drawing-room from the hall stood an old man, who had only just come in, and who, to judge by the expression of his downcast face and the shrug of his shoulders, was by no means pleased with Panshin's song, pretty though it was. After waiting a moment and flicking the dust off his boots with a coarse pocket-handkerchief, this man suddenly raised his eyes, compressed his lips with a morose expression, and his stooping figure bent forward, he entered the drawing-room.

'Ah! Christopher Fedoritch, how are you?' exclaimed Panshin before any of the others could speak, and he jumped up quickly from his seat. 'I had no suspicion that you were here, —nothing would have induced me to sing my song before you. I know you are no lover of light music.'

'I did not hear it,' declared the new-comer, in very bad

Russian, and exchanging greetings with everyone, he stood awkwardly in the middle of the room.

'Have you come, Monsieur Lemm,' said Marya Dmitrievna, 'to give Lisa her music lesson?'

'No, not Lisaveta Mihalovna, but Elena Mihalovna.'

'Oh! very well. Lenotchka, go upstairs with Mr Lemm.'

The old man was about to follow the little girl, but Panshin stopped him.

'Don't go after the lesson, Christopher Fedoritch,' he said. 'Lisaveta Mihalovna and I are going to play a duet of Beethoven's sonata.'

The old man muttered some reply, and Panshin continued in German, mispronouncing the words—

'Lisaveta Mihalovna showed me the religious cantata you dedicated to her—a beautiful thing! Pray, do not suppose that I cannot appreciate serious music—quite the contrary: it is tedious sometimes, but then it is very elevating.'

The old man crimsoned to his ears, and with a sidelong look at Lisa, he hurriedly went out of the room.

Marya Dmitrievna asked Panshin to sing his song again; but he protested that he did not wish to torture the ears of the musical German, and suggested to Lisa that they should attack Beethoven's sonata. Then Marya Dmitrievna heaved a sigh, and in her turn suggested to Gedeonovsky a walk in the garden. 'I should like,' she said, 'to have a little more talk, and to consult you about our poor Fedya.' Gedeonovsky bowed with a smirk, and with two fingers picked up his hat, on the brim of which his gloves had been tidily laid, and went away with Marya Dmitrievna. Panshin and Lisa remained alone in the room; she fetched the sonata, and opened it; both seated themselves at the piano in silence. Overhead were heard the faint sounds of scales, played by the uncertain fingers of Lenotchka.

* *5* *

Christopher Theodor Gottlieb Lemm was born in 1786 in the town of Chemnitz in Saxony. His parents were poor musicians. His father played the French horn, his mother the harp; he himself was practising on three different instruments by the time he was five. At eight years old he was left an orphan, and from his tenth year he began to earn his bread by his art. He led a wandering life for many years, and performed everywhere in restaurants, at fairs, at peasants' weddings, and at balls. At last he got into an orchestra, and constantly rising in it, he obtained the position of director. He was rather a poor performer; but he understood music thoroughly. At twenty-eight he migrated into Russia, on the invitation of a great nobleman, who did not care for music himself, but kept an orchestra for show. Lemm lived with him seven years in the capacity of orchestra conductor, and left him empty-handed. The nobleman was ruined, he intended to give him a promissory note, but in the sequel refused him even that—in short, did not pay him a farthing. He was advised to go away; but he was unwilling to return home in poverty from Russia, that great Russia which is a mine of gold for artists; he decided to remain and try his luck. For twenty years the poor German had been trying his luck; he had lived in various gentlemen's houses, had suffered and put up with much, had faced privation, had struggled like a fish on the ice; but the idea of returning to his own country never left him among all the hardships he endured; it was this dream alone that sustained him. But fate did not see fit to grant him this last and first happiness: at fifty, broken-down in health and prematurely aged, he drifted to the town of O——, and remained there for good, having now lost once for all every hope of leaving Russia, which he detested. He gained his poor livelihood somehow by lessons. Lemm's exterior was not prepossessing. He was short and bent, with crooked shoulders, and a contracted chest, with large flat feet, and bluish white nails on the gnarled bony fingers of his sinewy red hands. He had a wrinkled face, sunken cheeks, and compressed lips, which he was for ever twitching and biting; and this, together with his habitual taciturnity, produced an impression almost sinister. His grey hair hung in tufts on his low brow; like smouldering embers, his little set eyes glowed with dull fire. He moved painfully, at every step swinging his ungainly body forward. Some of his movements recalled the clumsy actions of an owl in a cage when it feels that it is being looked at, but itself can hardly see out of its great yellow eyes timorously and drowsily blinking. Pitiless, prolonged sorrow had laid its indelible stamp on the poor musician; it had disfigured and deformed his person, by no means attractive to begin with. But any one who was able to get over the first impression would have discerned something good, and honest, and out of the common in this half-shattered creature. A devoted admirer of Bach and Handel, a master of his art, gifted with a lively imagination and that boldness of conception which is only vouchsafed to the German race, Lemm might, in time— who knows?—have taken rank with the great composers of his fatherland, had his life been different; but he was born under an unlucky star! He had written much in his life, and it had not been granted to him to see one of his compositions produced; he did not know how to set about things in the right way, to gain favour in the right place, and to make a push at the right moment. A long, long time ago, his one friend and admirer, also a German and also poor, had published two of Lemm's sonatas at his own expense—the whole edition remained on the shelves of the music-shops; they disappeared without a trace, as though they had been thrown into a river by night. At last Lemm had renounced everything; the years too did their work; his mind had grown hard and stiff, as his fingers had stiffened. He lived alone in a little cottage not far from the Kalitin's house, with an old cook he had taken out of the poorhouse (he had never married). He took long walks, and read the Bible and the Protestant version of the Psalms, and Shakespeare in Schlegel's translation. He had composed nothing for a long time; but apparently, Lisa, his best pupil, had been able to inspire him; he had written for her the cantata to which Panshin had made allusion. The words of this cantata he had borrowed from his collection of hymns. He had added a few verses of his own. It was sung by two choruses—a chorus of the happy and a chorus of the unhappy. The two were brought into harmony at the end, and sang together, 'Merciful God, have pity on us sinners, and deliver us from all evil thoughts and earthly hopes.' On the title-page was the inscription, most carefully written and even illuminated, 'Only the righteous are justified.

[14]

A religious cantata. Composed and dedicated to Miss Elisa-veta Kalitin, his dear pupil, by her teacher, C. T. G. Lemm.'
The words, 'Only the righteous are justified' and 'Elisaveta Kalitin', were encircled by rays. Below was written: 'For you alone, *für Sie allein.*' This was why Lemm had grown red, and looked reproachfully at Lisa; he was deeply wounded when Panshin spoke of his cantata before him.

✳ 6 ✳

Panshin, who was playing bass, struck the first chords of the sonata loudly and decisively, but Lisa did not begin her part. He stopped and looked at her. Lisa's eyes were fixed directly on him, and expressed displeasure. There was no smile on her lips, her whole face looked stern and even mournful.

'What's the matter?' he asked.

'Why did you not keep your word?' she said. 'I showed you Christopher Fedoritch's cantata on the express condition that you said nothing about it to him?'

'I beg your pardon, Lisaveta Mihalovna, the words slipped out unawares.'

'You have hurt his feelings and mine too. Now he will not trust even me.'

'How could I help it, Lisaveta Mihalovna? Ever since I was a little boy I could never see a German without wanting to tease him.'

'How can you say that, Vladimir Nikolaitch? This German is poor, lonely, and broken-down—have you no pity for him? Can you wish to tease him?'

Panshin was a little taken aback.

'You are right, Lisaveta Mihalovna,' he declared. 'It's my everlasting thoughtlessness that's to blame. No, don't contra-dict me; I know myself. So much harm has come to me from my want of thought. It's owing to that failing that I am thought to be an egoist.'

Panshin paused. With whatever subject he began a con-versation, he generally ended by talking of himself, and the subject was changed by him so easily, so smoothly and genially, that it seemed unconscious.

'In your own household, for instance,' he went on, 'your mother certainly wishes me well, she is so kind; you—well, I don't know your opinion of me; but on the other hand your aunt simply can't bear me. I must have offended her too by some thoughtless, stupid speech. You know I'm not a favourite of hers, am I?'

'No,' Lisa admitted with some reluctance, 'she doesn't like you.'

Panshin ran his fingers quickly over the keys, and a scarcely perceptible smile glided over his lips.

'Well, and you?' he said, 'do you too think me an egoist?'

'I know you very little,' replied Lisa, 'but I don't consider you an egoist; on the contrary, I can't help feeling grateful to you.'

'I know, I know what you mean to say,' Panshin interrupted, and again he ran his fingers over the keys: 'for the music and the books I bring you, for the wretched sketches with which I adorn your album, and so forth. I might do all that—and be an egoist all the same. I venture to think that you don't find me a bore, and don't think me a bad fellow, but still you suppose that I—what's the saying?—would sacrifice friend or father for the sake of a witticism.'

'You are careless and forgetful, like all men of the world,' observed Lisa, 'that is all.'

Panshin frowned a little.

'Come,' he said, 'don't let us discuss me any more; let us play our sonata. There's only one thing I must beg of you,' he added, smoothing out the leaves of the book on the music stand, 'think what you like of me, call me an egoist even—so be it! but don't call me a man of the world; that name's insufferable to me. . . . *Anch 'io sono pittore.* I too am an artist, though a poor one—and *that*—I mean that I'm a poor artist, I shall show directly. Let us begin.'

'Very well, let us begin,' said Lisa.

The first *adagio* went fairly successfully though Panshin made more than one false note. His own compositions and what he had practised thoroughly he played very nicely, but he played at sight badly. So the second part of the sonata—a rather quick *allegro*—broke down completely; at the twentieth bar, Panshin, who was two bars behind, gave in, and pushed his chair back with a laugh.

'No!' he cried, 'I can't play to-day; it's a good thing Lemm did not hear us; he would have had a fit.'

Lisa got up, shut the piano, and turned round to Panshin. 'What are we going to do?' she asked.

'That's just like you, that question! You can never sit with your hands idle. Well, if you like let us sketch, since it's not quite dark. Perhaps the other muse, the muse of painting—what was her name? I have forgotten . . . will be more propitious to me. Where's your album? I remember, my landscape there is not finished.'

Lisa went into the other room to fetch the album, and Panshin, left alone, drew a cambric handkerchief out of his pocket, rubbed his nails and looked as it were critically at his hands. He had beautiful white hands; on the second finger of his left hand he wore a spiral gold ring. Lisa came back; Panshin sat down at the window, and opened the album.

'Ah!' he exclaimed: 'I see that you have begun to copy my landscape—and capitally too. Excellent! only just here—give me a pencil—the shadows are not put in strongly enough. Look.'

And Panshin with a flourish added a few long strokes. He was for ever drawing the same landscape: in the foreground large dishevelled trees, a stretch of meadow in the background, and jagged mountains on the horizon. Lisa looked over his shoulders at his work.

'In drawing, just as in life generally,' observed Panshin, holding his head to right and to left, 'lightness and boldness—are the great things.'

At that instant Lemm came into the room, and with a stiff bow was about to leave it; but Panshin, throwing aside album and pencils, placed himself in his way.

'Where are you going, dear Christopher Fedoritch? Aren't you going to stay and have tea with us?'

'I go home,' answered Lemm in a surly voice; 'my head aches.'

'Oh, what nonsense!—do stop. We'll have an argument about Shakespeare.'

[17]

'My head aches,' repeated the old man.

'We set to work on the sonata of Beethoven without you,' continued Panshin, taking hold of him affectionately and smiling brightly, 'but we couldn't get on at all. Fancy, I couldn't play two notes together correctly.'

'You'd better have sung your song again,' replied Lemm, removing Panshin's hands, and he walked away.

Lisa ran after him. She overtook him on the stairs.

'Christopher Fedoritch, I want to tell you,' she said to him in German, accompanying him over the short green grass of the yard to the gate, 'I did wrong—forgive me.'

Lemm made no answer.

'I showed Vladimir Nikolaitch your cantata; I felt sure he would appreciate it,—and he did like it very much, really.'

Lemm stopped.

'It's no matter,' he said in Russian, and then added in his own language, 'but he cannot understand anything; how is it you don't see that? He's a dilettante—and that's all!'

'You are unjust to him,' replied Lisa, 'he understands everything, and he can do almost everything himself.'

'Yes, everything second-rate, cheap, scamped work. That pleases, and he pleases, and he is glad it is so—and so much the better. I'm not angry; the cantata and I —we are a pair of old fools; I'm a little ashamed, but it's no matter.'

'Forgive me, Christopher Fedoritch,' Lisa said again.

'It's no matter,' he repeated again in Russian, 'you're a good girl . . . but here is someone coming to see you. Good-bye. You are a very good girl.'

And Lemm moved with hastened steps towards the gate, through which had entered some gentleman unknown to him in a grey coat and a wide straw hat. Bowing politely to him (he always saluted all new faces in the town of O——; from acquaintances he always turned aside in the street—that was the rule he had laid down for himself), Lemm passed by and disappeared behind the fence. The stranger looked after him in amazement, and after gazing attentively at Lisa, went straight up to her.

'You don't recognise me,' he said, taking off his hat, 'but I recognised you in spite of its being seven years since I saw you last. You were a child then. I am Lavretsky. Is your mother at home? Can I see her?'

'Mamma will be glad to see you,' replied Lisa; 'she had heard of your arrival.'

'Let me see, I think your name is Elisaveta?' said Lavretsky, as he went up the stairs.

'Yes.'

'I remember you very well; you had even then a face one doesn't forget. I used to bring you sweets in those days.'

Lisa blushed and thought what a queer man. Lavretsky stopped for an instant in the hall. Lisa went into the drawing-room, where Panshin's voice and laugh could be heard; he had been communicating some gossip of the town to Marya Dmitrievna, and Gedeonovsky, who by this time had come in from the garden, and he was himself laughing aloud at the story he was telling. At the name of Lavretsky, Marya Dmitrievna was all in a flutter. She turned pale and went up to meet him.

'How do you do, how do you do, my dear cousin?' she cried in a plaintive and almost tearful voice, 'how glad I am to see you!'

'How are you, cousin?' replied Lavretsky, with a friendly pressure of her out-stretched hand; 'how has Providence been treating you?'

'Sit down, sit down, my dear Fedor Ivanitch. Ah, how glad I am! But let me present my daughter Lisa to you.'

'I have already introduced myself to Lisaveta Mihalovna,' interposed Lavretsky.

'Monsieur Panshin . . . Sergei Petrovitch Gedeonovsky . . . Please sit down. When I look at you, I can hardly believe my eyes. How are you?'

'As you see; I'm flourishing. And you, too, cousin—no ill-luck to you!—have grown no thinner in eight years.'

'To think how long it is since we met!' observed Marya Dmitrievna dreamily. 'Where have you come from now?

Where did you leave . . . that is, I meant to say,' she put in hastily, 'I meant to say, are you going to be with us for long?'

'I have come now from Berlin,' replied Lavretsky, 'and tomorrow I shall go into the country—probably for a long time.'

'You will live at Lavriky, I suppose?'

'No, not at Lavriky; I have a little place, twenty miles from here: I am going there.'

'Is that the little estate that came to you from Glafira Petrovna?'

'Yes.'

'Really, Fedor Ivanitch! You have such a magnificent house at Lavriky.'

Lavretsky knitted his brows a little.

'Yes . . . but there's a small lodge in this little property, and I need nothing more for a time. That place is the most convenient for me now.'

Marya Dmitrievna was again thrown into such a state of agitation that she became quite stiff, and her hands hung lifeless by her sides. Panshin came to her support by entering into conversation with Lavretsky. Marya Dmitrievna regained her composure, she leaned back in her arm-chair and now and then put in a word. But she looked all the while with such sympathy at her guest, sighed so significantly, and shook her head so dejectedly, that the latter at last lost patience and asked her rather sharply if she was unwell.

'Thank God, no,' replied Marya Dmitrievna; 'why do you ask?'

'Oh, I fancied you didn't seem to be quite yourself.'

Marya Dmitrievna assumed a dignified and somewhat offended air. 'If that's how the land lies,' she thought, 'it's absolutely no matter to me; I see, my good fellow, it's all like water on a duck's back for you; any other man would have wasted away with grief, but you've grown fat on it.' Marya Dmitrievna did not mince matters in her own mind: she expressed herself with more elegance aloud.

Lavretsky certainly did not look like the victim of fate. His rosy-cheeked typical Russian face, with its large white brow, rather thick nose, and wide straight lips seemed breathing with the wild health of the steppes, with vigorous primaeval energy. He was splendidly well-built, and his fair curly hair stood up on his head like a boy's. It was only in his blue eyes, with their over-hanging brows and somewhat fixed look, that one could trace an expression, not exactly of melancholy, nor exactly of weariness, and his voice had almost too measured a cadence.

Panshin meanwhile continued to keep up the conversation. He turned it upon the profits of sugar-boiling, on which he had lately read two French pamphlets, and with modest composure undertook to expound their contents, without mentioning, however, a single word about the source of his information.

'Good God, it is Fedya!' came through the half-opened door the voice of Marfa Timofyevna in the next room. 'Fedya himself!' and the old woman ran hurriedly into the room. Lavretsky had not time to get up from his seat before she had him in her arms. 'Let me have a look at you,' she said, holding his face off at arm's length. 'Ah! What a splendid fellow you are! You've grown older a little, but not a bit changed for the worse, upon my word! But why are you kissing my hands—kiss my face if you're not afraid of my wrinkled cheeks. You never asked after me—whether your aunt was alive—I warrant: and you were in my arms as soon as you were born, you great rascal! Well, that is nothing to you, I suppose; why should you remember me? But it was a good idea of yours to come back. And pray,' she added, turning to Marya Dmitrievna, 'have you offered him something to eat'?

'I don't want anything,' Lavretsky hastened to declare.

'Come, you must at least have some tea, my dear. Lord have mercy on us! He has come from I don't know where, and they don't even give him a cup of tea! Lisa, run and stir them up, and make haste. I remember he was dreadfully greedy when he was a little fellow, and he likes good things now, I daresay.'

'My respects, Marfa Timofyevna,' said Panshin, approaching the delighted old lady from one side with a low bow.

'Pardon me, sir,' replied Marfa Timofyevna, 'for not observing you in my delight. You have grown like your mother, the poor darling,' she went on, turning again to Lavretsky, 'but your nose was always your father's, and your father's it has remained. Well, and are you going to be with us for long?'

'I am going to-morrow, aunt.'

'Where?'

'Home to Vassilyevskoe.'

'To-morrow?'

'Yes, to-morrow.'

'Well, if to-morrow it must be. God bless you—you know best. Only mind you come and say good-bye to me.' The old woman patted his cheek. 'I did not think I should be here to see you; not that I have made up my mind to die yet a while—I shall last another ten years, I daresay: all we Pestovs live long; your late grandfather used to say we had two lives; but you see there was no telling how much longer you were going to dangle about abroad. Well, you're a fine lad, a fine lad; can you lift twenty stone with one hand as you used to do, eh? Your late papa was fantastical in some things, if I may say so; but he did well in having that Swiss to bring you up; do you remember you used to fight with your fists with him?—gymnastics, wasn't it they called it? But there, why I am gabbling away like this; I have only been hindering Mr Panshín (she never prononounced his name Pánshin as was correct) from holding forth. Besides, we'd better go and have tea; yes, let's go on to the terrace, my boy, and drink it there; we have some real cream, not like what you get in your Londons and Parises. Come along, come along, and you, Fedusha, give me your arm. Oh! but what an arm it is! Upon my word, no fear of my stumbling with you!'

Everyone got up and went out on to the terrace, except Gedeonovsky, who quietly took his departure. During the whole of Lavretsky's conversation with Marya Dmitrievna, Panshin, and Marfa Timofyevna, he sat in a corner, blinking attentively, with an open mouth of childish curiosity; now he was in haste to spread the news of the new arrival through the town.

At eleven o'clock on the evening of the same day, this is what was happening in Madame Kalitin's house. Downstairs, Vladimir Nikolaitch, seizing a favourable moment, was taking leave of Lisa at the drawing-room door, and saying to her, as he held her hand, 'You know who it is draws me here; you know why I am constantly coming to your house; what need of words when all is clear as it is?' Lisa did not speak, and looked on the ground, without smiling, with her brows slightly contracted, and a flush on her cheek, but she did not draw away her hands. While up-stairs, in Marfa Timofyevna's room, by the light of a little lamp hanging before the tarnished old holy images, Lavretsky was sitting in a low chair, his elbows on his knees and his face buried in his hands; the old woman, standing before him, now and then silently stroked his hair. He spent more than an hour with her, after taking leave of his hostess; he had scarcely said anything to his kind old friend, and she did not question him. . . . Indeed, what need to speak, what was there to ask? Without that she understood all, and felt for everything of which his heart was full.

✳ 8 ✳

Fedor Ivanitch Lavretsky—we must ask the reader's permission to break off the thread of our story for a time—came of an old noble family. The founder of the house of Lavretsky came over from Prussia in the reign of Vassili the Blind, and received a grant of two hundred *chetverts* of land in Byezhetsk. Many of his descendants filled various offices, and served under princes and persons of eminence in outlying districts, but not one of them rose above the rank of an inspector of the Imperial table nor acquired any considerable fortune. The richest and most distinguished of all the Lavretskys was Fedor Ivanitch's great-grandfather, Andrei, a man cruel and daring, cunning and able. Even to this day stories still linger of his tyranny, his savage temper, his reckless munificence, and his insatiable avarice. He was very stout and tall, swarthy of countenance and beardless, he spoke in a thick voice and seemed half asleep; but the more quietly he spoke, the more those about him trembled. He had managed to get a wife who was a fit match for him. She was a gipsy by birth, goggle-eyed and hook-nosed, with a round yellow face. She was irascible and vindictive, and never gave way in anything to her husband, who almost killed her, and whose death she did not survive, though she had been for ever quarrelling with him. The son of Andrei, Piotr, Fedor's grandfather, did not take after his father; he was a typical landowner of the steppes, rather a simpleton, loud-voiced, but slow to move, coarse but not ill-natured, hospitable and very fond of coursing with dogs. He was over thirty when he inherited from his father a property of two thousand serfs in capital condition; but he had soon dissipated it, and had partly mortgaged his estate, and demoralised his servants. All sorts of people of low position, known and unknown, came crawling like cockroaches from all parts into his spacious, warm, ill-kept halls. All this mass of people ate what they could get, but always had their fill, drank till they were drunk, and carried off what they could, praising and blessing their genial host; and their host too, when he was out of humour, blessed his guests—for a pack of sponging toadies, but he was bored when he was without them. Piotr Andreitch's wife was a meek-spirited creature; he had taken her from a neighbouring family by his father's choice and command; her name was Anna Pavlovna. She never interfered in anything, welcomed guests cordially, and readily paid visits herself, though being powdered, she used to declare, would be the death of her. 'They put,' she used to say in her old age, 'a fox's brush on your head, comb all the hair up over it, smear it with grease, and dust it over with flour, and stick it up with iron pins,—there's no washing it off afterwards; but to pay visits without powder was quite impossible—people would be offended. Ah, it was a torture!'

She liked being driven with fast-trotting horses, and was ready to play cards from morning till evening, and would always keep the score of the pennies she had lost or won hidden under her hand when her husband came near the card-table; but all her dowry, her whole fortune, she had put absolutely at his disposal. She bore him two children, a son Ivan, the father of Fedor, and a daughter Glafira. Ivan was not brought up at home, but lived with a rich old maiden aunt, the Princess Kubensky; she had fixed on him for her heir (but for that his father would not have let him go). She dressed him up like a doll, engaged all kinds of teachers for him, and put him in charge of a tutor, a Frenchman, who had been an abbé, a pupil of Jean-Jacques Rousseau, a certain M. Courtin de Vaucelles, a subtle and wily intriguer—the very, as she expressed it, *fine fleur* of emigration—and finished at almost seventy years old by marrying this '*fine fleur*', and making over all her property to him. Soon afterwards, covered with rouge, and redolent of perfume *à la Richelieu*, surrounded by negro boys, delicate-shaped greyhounds and shrieking parrots, she died on a crooked silken divan of the time of Louis XV, with an enamelled snuff-box of Petitot's workmanship in her hand—and died, deserted by her husband; the insinuating M. Courtin had preferred to remove to Paris with her money. Ivan had only reached his twentieth year when this unexpected blow (we mean the princess's marriage, not her death) fell upon him; he did not care to stay in his aunt's house, where he found himself suddenly transformed from a wealthy heir to a poor relation; the society in Petersburg in which he had grown up was closed to him; he felt an aversion for entering the government service in the lower grades, with nothing but hard work and obscurity before him, —this was at the very beginning of the reign of the Emperor Alexander. He was obliged reluctantly to return to the country to his father. How squalid, poor, and wretched his parents' home seemed to him! The stagnation and sordidness of life in the country offended him at every step. He was consumed with *ennui*. Moreover, everyone in the house, except his mother, looked at him with unfriendly eyes. His father did not like his town manners, his swallow-tail coats, his frilled shirt-front, his books, his flute, his fastidious ways, in which he detected—not incorrectly—a disgust for his surroundings; he was for ever complaining and grumbling at his son. 'Nothing here,' he used to say, 'is to his taste; at table he is all in a fret, and doesn't eat; he can't bear the heat and close smell of the room; the sight of folks drunk upsets him, one daren't beat any one before him; he doesn't want to go into the government service; he's weakly, as you see, in health; fie upon him, the milksop! And all this because he's got his head full of Voltaire.' The old man had a special dislike to Voltaire, and the 'fanatic' Diderot, though he had not read a word of their works; reading was not in his line. Piotr

Andreitch was not mistaken; his son's head for that matter was indeed full of both Diderot and Voltaire, and not only of them alone, of Rousseau too, and Helvetius, and many other writers of the same kind—but they were in his head only. The retired abbé and encyclopédist who had been Ivan Petrovitch's tutor had taken pleasure in pouring all the wisdom of the eighteenth century into his pupil, and he was simply brimming over with it; it was there in him, but without mixing in his blood, nor penetrating to his soul, nor shaping itself in any firm convictions. . . . But, indeed, could one expect convictions from a young man of fifty years ago, when even at the present day we have not succeeded in attaining them? The guests, too, who frequented his father's house, were oppressed by Ivan Petrovitch's presence; he regarded them with loathing, they were afraid of him; and with his sister Glafira, who was twelve years older than he, he could not get on at all. This Glafira was a strange creature; she was ugly, crooked, and spare, with severe, wide-open eyes, and thin compressed lips. In her face, her voice, and her quick angular movements, she took after her grandmother, the gipsy, Andrei's wife. Obstinate and fond of power, she would not even hear of marriage. The return of Ivan Petrovitch did not fit in with her plans; while the Princess Kubensky kept him with her, she had hoped to receive at least half of her father's estate; in her avarice, too, she was like her grandmother. Besides, Glafira envied her brother, he was so well educated, spoke such good French with a Parisian accent, while she was scarcely able to pronounce 'bon jour' or 'comment vous portez-vous?' To be sure, her parents did not know any French, but that was no comfort to her. Ivan Petrovitch did not know what to do with himself for wretchedness and *ennui*; he had spent hardly a year in the country, but that year seemed to him as long as ten. The only consolation he could find was in talking to his mother, and he would sit for whole hours in her low-pitched rooms, listening to the good woman's simple-hearted prattle, and eating preserves. It so happened that among Anna Pavlovna's maids there was one very pretty girl with clear soft eyes and refined features, Malanya by name, a modest intelligent creature. She took his fancy at first sight, and he fell in love with her: he fell in love with her timid movements, her bashful answers, her gentle voice and gentle smile; every day she seemed sweeter to him. And she became devoted to Ivan Petrovitch with all the strength of her soul, as none but Russian girls can be devoted—and she gave herself to him. In the large household of a country squire nothing can long be kept a secret; soon everyone knew of the love between the young master and Malanya; the gossip even reached the ears of Piotr Andreitch himself. Under other circumstances, he would probably have paid no attention to a matter of so little importance, but he had long had a grudge against his son, and was delighted at an opportunity of humiliating the town-bred wit and dandy. A storm of fuss and clamour was raised; Malanya was locked up in the pantry, Ivan Petrovitch was summoned into his father's presence. Anna Pavlovna too ran up at the hubbub. She began trying to pacify her husband, but Piotr Andreitch would hear nothing. He pounced down like a hawk on his son, reproached him with immorality, with godlessness, with hypocrisy; he took the opportunity to vent on him all the wrath against the Princess Kubensky that had been simmering within him, and lavished abusive epithets upon him. At first Ivan Petrovitch was silent and held himself in, but when his father thought fit to threaten him with a shameful punishment he could endure it no longer. 'Ah', he thought, 'the fanatic Diderot is brought out again, then I will take the bull by the horns, I will astonish you all.' And thereupon with a calm and even voice, though quaking inwardly in every limb, Ivan Petrovitch declared to his father, that there was no need to reproach him with immorality; that though he did not intend to justify his fault he was ready to make amends for it, the more willingly as he felt himself to be superior to every kind of prejudice—and in fact—was ready to marry Malanya. In uttering these words Ivan Petrovitch did undoubtedly attain his object; he so astonished Piotr Andreitch that the latter stood open-eyed, and was struck dumb for a moment; but instantly he came to himself, and just as he was, in a dressing-gown bordered with squirrel fur and slippers on his bare feet, he flew at Ivan Petrovitch with his fists. The latter, as though by design, had that morning arranged his locks *à la Titus*, and put on a new English coat of a blue colour, high boots with little tassels and very tight modish buckskin breeches.

Anna Pavlovna shrieked with all her might and covered her face with her hands; but her son ran over the whole house, dashed out into the courtyard, rushed into the kitchen-garden, into the pleasure-grounds, and flew across into the road, and kept running without looking round till at last he ceased to hear the heavy tramp of his father's steps behind him and his shouts, jerked out with effort. 'Stop you scoundrel!' he cried, 'stop! or I will curse you!' Ivan Petrovitch took refuge with a neighbour, a small landowner, and Piotr Andreitch returned home worn out and perspiring, and without taking breath, announced that he should deprive his son of his blessing and inheritance, gave orders that all his foolish books should be burnt, and that the girl Malanya should be sent to a distant village without loss of time. Some kind-hearted people found out Ivan Petrovitch and let him know everything. Humiliated and driven to fury, he vowed he would be revenged on his father, and the same night lay in wait for the peasant's cart in which Malanya was being driven away, carried her off by force, galloped off to the nearest town with her and married her. He was supplied with money by the neighbour, a good-natured retired marine officer, a confirmed tippler, who took an intense delight in every kind of—as he expressed it—romantic story. The next day Ivan Petrovitch wrote an ironically cold and polite letter to Piotr Andreitch, and set off to the village where lived his second cousin, Dmitri Pestov, with his sister, already known to the reader, Marfa Timofyevna. He told them all, announced his intention to go to Petersburg to try to obtain a post there, and besought them, at least for a time, to give his wife a home. At the word 'wife' he shed tears, and in spite of his city breeding and philosophy he bowed himself in humble, supplicating Russian fashion at his relations' feet, and even touched the ground with his forehead. The Pestovs, kind-hearted and compassionate people, readily agreed to his request. He stayed with them for three weeks, secretly expecting a reply from his father; but no reply came—and there was no chance of a reply coming. Piotr Andreitch, on hearing of his son's marriage, took to his bed, and forbade Ivan Petrovitch's name to be mentioned before him; but his mother, without her husband's knowledge, borrowed from the rector, and sent 500 roubles and a little image

to his wife. She was afraid to write, but sent a message to
Ivan Petrovitch by a lean peasant, who could walk fifty miles
a day, that he was not to take it too much to heart; that, please
God, all would be arranged, and his father's wrath would be
turned to kindness; that she too would have preferred a different daughter-in-law, but that she sent Malanya Sergyevna her
motherly blessing. The lean peasant received a rouble, asked
permission to see the new young mistress, to whom he happened to be godfather, kissed her hand and ran off at his best
speed.

And Ivan Petrovitch set off to Petersburg with a light heart.
An unknown future awaited him; poverty perhaps menaced
him, but he had broken away from the country life he detested,
and above all, he had not been false to his teachers, he had
actually put into practice the doctrines of Rousseau, Diderot,
and *la Déclaration des droits de l'homme*. A sense of having
done his duty, of triumph, and of pride filled his soul; and
indeed the separation from his wife did not greatly afflict him;
he would have been more perturbed by the necessity of being
constantly with her. That deed was done, now he wanted to
set about doing something fresh. In Petersburg, contrary to
his own expectations, he met with success; the Princess
Kubensky, whom Monsieur Courtin had by that time deserted, but who was still living, in order to make up in some
way to her nephew for having wronged him, gave him intro-
ductions to all her friends, and presented him with 5,000
roubles—almost all that remained of her money—and a
Lepikovsky watch with his monogram encircled by Cupids.
Three months had not passed before he obtained a position in
a Russian embassy to London, and in the first English vessel
that sailed (steamers were not even talked of then) he crossed
the sea. A few months later he received a letter from Pestov.
The good-natured landowner congratulated Ivan Petrovitch
on the birth of a son, who had been born into the world in the
village of Pokrovskoe on the 20th of August 1807, and named
Fedor, in honour of the holy martyr Fedor Stratilat. On
account of her extreme weakness Malanya Sergyevna added
only a few lines; but these few lines were a surprise, for Ivan
Petrovitch had not known that Marfa Timofyevna had
taught his wife to read and write. Ivan Petrovitch did not long

abandon himself to the sweet emotion of parental feeling; he was dancing attendance on a notorious Phryne or Lais of the day (classical names were still in vogue at that date); the Peace of Tilsit had only just been concluded and all the world was hurrying after pleasure, in a giddy whirl of dissipation, and his head had been turned by the black eyes of a bold beauty. He had very little money, but he was lucky at cards, made many acquaintances, took part in all entertainments, in a word, he was in the swim.

* 9 *

For a long time the old Lavretsky could not forgive his son for his marriage. If six months later Ivan Petrovitch had come to him with a penitent face and had thrown himself at his feet, he would, very likely, have pardoned him, after giving him a pretty severe scolding, and a tap with his stick by way of intimidating him, but Ivan Petrovitch went on living abroad and apparently did not care a straw. 'Be silent! I dare you to speak of it,' Piotr Andreitch said to his wife every time she ventured to try to incline him to mercy. 'The puppy, he ought to thank God for ever that I have not laid my curse upon him; my father would have killed him, the worthless scamp, with his own hands, and he would have done right too.' At such terrible speeches Anna Pavlovna could only cross herself secretly. As for Ivan Petrovitch's wife, Piotr Andreitch at first would not even hear her name, and in answer to a letter of Pestov's, in which he mentioned his daughter-in-law, he went so far as to send him word that he knew nothing of any daughter-in-law, and that it was forbidden by law to harbour run-away wenches, a fact which he thought it his duty to remind him of. But later on, he was softened by hearing of the birth of a grandson, and he gave orders secretly that inquiries should be made about the health of the mother, and sent her a little money, also as though it did not come from him. Fedya was not a year old before Anna Pavlovna fell ill with a fatal complaint. A few days before her end, when she could no longer leave her bed, with timid tears in her eyes, fast growing dim, she informed her husband in the presence of the priest that she wanted to see her daughter-in-law and bid her farewell, and to give her grandchild her blessing. The heartbroken old man soothed her, and at once sent off his own carriage for his daughter-in-law, for the first time giving her the title of Malanya Sergyevna. Malanya came with her son and Marfa Timofyevna, who would not on any consideration allow her to go alone, and was unwilling to expose her to any indignity. Half dead with fright, Malanya Sergyevna went into Piotr Andreitch's room. A nurse followed, carrying Fedya. Piotr Andreitch looked at her without speaking; she went up to kiss his hand; her trembling lips were only just able to touch it with a silent kiss.

'Well, my upstart lady,' he brought out at last, 'how do you do? Let us go to the mistress.'

He got up and bent over Fedya; the baby smiled and held out his little white hands to him. This changed the old man's mood.

'Ah,' he said, 'poor little one, you were pleading for your father; I will not abandon you, little bird.'

Directly Malanya Sergyevna entered Anna Pavlovna's bedroom, she fell on her knees near the door. Anna Pavlovna beckoned her to come to her bedside, embraced her, and blessed her son; then turning a face contorted by cruel suffering to her husband she made an effort to speak.

'I know, I know, what you want to ask,' said Piotr Andreitch; 'don't fret yourself, she shall stay with us, and I will forgive Vanka for her sake.'

With an effort Anna Pavlovna took her husband's hand and pressed it to her lips. The same evening she breathed her last.

Piotr Andreitch kept his word. He informed his son that for the sake of his mother's dying hours, and for the sake of the little Fedor, he sent him his blessing and was keeping Malanya Sergyevna in his house. Two rooms on the ground floor were devoted to her; he presented her to his most honoured guests, the one-eyed brigadier Skurehin, and his wife, and bestowed on her two waiting-maids and a page for errands. Marfa Timofyevna took leave of her; she detested Glafira, and in the course of one day had fallen out with her three times.

It was a painful and embarrassing position at first for poor Malanya, but, after a while, she learnt to bear it, and grew used to her father-in-law. He, too, grew accustomed to her, and even fond of her, though he scarcely ever spoke to her, and a certain involuntary contempt was perceptible even in his signs of affection to her. Malanya Sergyevna had most to put up with from her sister-in-law. Even during her mother's lifetime, Glafira had succeeded by degrees in getting the whole household into her hands; everyone, from her father, downwards, submitted to her rule; not a piece of sugar was given out without her sanction; she would rather have died than shared her authority with another mistress—and with such a mistress! Her brother's marriage had incensed her even more than Piotr Andreitch; she set herself to give the upstart a lesson, and Malanya Sergyevna from the very first hour was her slave. And, indeed, how was she to contend against the masterful, haughty Glafira, submissive, constantly bewildered, timid, and weak in health as she was? Not a day passed without Glafira reminding her of her former position, and commending her for not forgetting herself. Malanya Sergyevna could have reconciled herself readily to these reminiscences and commendations, however bitter they might be—but Fedya was taken away from her, that was what crushed her. On the pretext that she was not capable of undertaking his education, she was scarcely allowed to see him; Glafira set herself to that task; the child was put absolutely under her control. Malanya Sergevna began, in her distress, to beseech Ivan Petrovitch, in her letters, to return home soon. Piotr Andreitch himself wanted to see his son, but Ivan Petrovitch did nothing but write. He thanked his father on his wife's account, and for the money sent him, promised to return quickly—and did not come. The year 1812 at last summoned him home from abroad. When they met again, after six years' absence, the father embraced his son, and not by a single word made allusion to their former differences; it was not a time for that now, all Russia was rising up against the enemy, and both of them felt that they had Russian blood in their veins. Piotr Andreitch equipped a whole regiment of volunteers at his own expense. But the war came to an end, the danger was over; Ivan Petrovitch began to be bored again, and again he felt drawn away to the distance, to the world in which he had grown up, and where he felt himself at home. Malanya Sergyevna could not keep him; she meant too little to him. Even her fondest hopes came to nothing; her husband considered that it was much more suitable to entrust Fedya's education to Glafira. Ivan Petrovitch's poor wife could not bear this blow, she could not bear a second separation; in a few days, without a murmur, she quietly passed away. All her life she had never been able to oppose anything, and she did not struggle against her illness. When she could no longer speak, when the shadows of death were already on her face, her features expressed, as of old, bewildered resignation and constant, uncomplaining meekness; with the same dumb submissiveness she looked at Glafira, and just as Anna Pavlovna kissed her husband's hand on her deathbed, she kissed Glafira's, commending to her, to Glafira, her only son. So ended the earthly existence of this good and gentle creature, torn, God knows why, like an uprooted tree from its natural soil and at once thrown down with its roots in the air; she had faded and passed away, leaving no trace, and no one mourned for her. Malanya Sergyevna's maids pitied her, and so did even Piotr Andreitch. The old man missed her silent presence. 'Forgive me . . . farewell, my meek one!' he whispered, as he took leave of her the last time in church. He wept as he threw a handful of earth in the grave.

He did not survive her long, not more than five years. In the winter of the year 1819, he died peacefully in Moscow, where he had moved with Glafira and his grandson, and left instructions that he should be buried beside Anna Pavlovna and 'Malasha'. Ivan Petrovitch was then in Paris amusing himself; he had retired from service soon after 1815. When he heard of his father's death he decided to return to Russia. It was necessary to make arrangements for the management of the property. Fedya, according to Glafira's letter, had reached his twelfth year, and the time had come to set about his education in earnest.

* *10* *

Ivan Petrovitch returned to Russia an Anglomaniac. His short-cropped hair, his starched shirt-front, his long-skirted pea-green overcoat with its multitude of capes, the sour expression of his face, something abrupt and at the same time indifferent in his behaviour, his way of speaking through his teeth, his sudden wooden laugh, the absence of smiles, his exclusively political or politico-economical conversation, his passion for roast beef and port wine—everything about him breathed, so to speak, of Great Britain. But, marvellous to relate, while he had been transformed into an Anglomaniac, Ivan Petrovitch had at the same time become a patriot, at least he called himself a patriot, though he knew Russia little, had not retained a single Russian habit, and expressed himself in Russian rather queerly; in ordinary conversation, his language was spiritless and inanimate and constantly interspersed with Gallicisms.

Ivan Petrovitch brought with him a few schemes in manuscript, relating to the administration and reform of the government; he was much displeased with everything he saw; the lack of system especially aroused his spleen. On his meeting with his sister, at the first word he announced to her that he was determined to introduce radical reforms, that henceforth everything to do with him would be on a different system. Glafira Petrovna made no reply to Ivan Petrovitch; she only ground her teeth and thought: 'Where am I to take refuge?' After she was back in the country, however, with her brother and nephew, her fears were soon set at rest. In the house, certainly, some changes were made; idlers and dependants met with summary dismissal; among them two old women were made to suffer, one blind, another broken down by paralysis; and also a decrepit major of the days of Catherine, who, on account of his really abnormal appetite, was fed on nothing but black bread and lentils. The order went forth not to admit the guests of former days; they were replaced by a distant neighbour, a certain fair-haired, scrofulous baron, a very well educated and very stupid man. New furniture was brought from Moscow; spittoons were introduced, and bells and

washing-stands; and breakfast began to be served in a different way; foreign wines replaced vodka and syrups, the servants were put into new livery; a motto was added to the
family arms: *in recto virtus.* . . . In reality, Glafira's power
suffered no diminution; the giving out and buying of stores
still depended on her. The Alsatian steward, brought from
abroad, tried to fight it out with her and lost his place, in spite
of the master's protection. As for the management of the
house, and the administration of the estates, Glafira Petrovna
had undertaken these duties also; in spite of Ivan Petrovitch's
intention,—more than once expressed—to breathe new life
into this chaos, everything remained as before; only the rent
was in some places raised, the mistress was more strict, and
the peasants were forbidden to apply direct to Ivan Petrovitch. The patriot had already a great contempt for his fellow-
countrymen. Ivan Petrovitch's system was applied in its full
force only to Fedya; his education really underwent a 'radical
reformation'; his father devoted himself exclusively to it.

* *11* *

Until Ivan Petrovitch's return from abroad, Fedya was, as
already related, in the hands of Glafira Petrovna. He was not
eight years old when his mother died; he did not see her
every day, and loved her passionately; the memory of her, of
her pale and gentle face, of her dejected looks and timid caresses, were imprinted on his heart for ever; but he vaguely
understood her position in the house; he felt that between him
and her there existed a barrier which she dared not and could
not break down. He was shy of his father, and, indeed, Ivan
Petrovitch on his side never caressed him; his grandfather
patted him on the head and gave him his hand to kiss, but he
thought him and called him a little fool. After the death of
Malanya Sergyevna, his aunt finally got him under her control. Fedya was afraid of her: he was afraid of her bright sharp
eyes and her harsh voice; he dared not utter a sound in her
presence; often, when he only moved a little in his chair, she

would hiss out at once: 'What are you doing? Sit still.' On Sundays, after mass, he was allowed to play, that is to say, he was given a thick book, a mysterious book, the work of a certain Maximovitch-Ambodik, entitled *Symbols and Emblems*. This book was a medley of about a thousand mostly very enigmatical pictures, and as many enigmatical interpretations of them in five languages. Cupid—naked and very puffy in the body—played a leading part in these illustrations. In one of them, under the heading, 'Saffron and the Rainbow', the interpretation appended was: 'Of this, the influence is vast'; opposite another, entitled 'A heron, flying with a violet in his beak', stood the inscription: 'To thee they are all known'. 'Cupid and the bear licking his fur' was inscribed, 'Little by little'. Fedya used to ponder over these pictures; he knew them all to the minutest details; some of them, always the same ones, used to set him dreaming, and afforded him food for meditation; he knew no other amusements. When the time came to teach him languages and music, Glafira Petrovna engaged, for next to nothing, an old maid, a Swede, with eyes like a hare's, who spoke French and German with mistakes in every alternate word, played after a fashion on the piano, and above all, salted cucumbers to perfection. In the society of this governess, his aunt, and the old servant maid, Vassilyevna, Fedya spent four whole years. Often he would sit in the corner with his 'Emblems'; he sat there endlessly; there was a scent of geranium in the low-pitched room, the solitary candle burnt dim, the cricket chirped monotonously, as though it were weary, the little clock ticked away hurriedly on the wall, a mouse scratched stealthily and gnawed at the wall-paper, and the three old women, like the Fates, swiftly and silently plied their knitting-needles, the shadows raced after their hands and quivered strangely in the half darkness, and strange, half-dark ideas swarmed in the child's brain. No one would have called Fedya an interesting child; he was rather pale, but stout, clumsily built and awkward—a thorough peasant, as Glafira Petrovna said; the pallor would soon have vanished from his cheeks, if he had been allowed oftener to be in the open air. He learnt fairly quickly, though he was often lazy; he never cried, but at times he was overtaken by a fit of savage obstinacy; then no one could soften him. Fedya loved no one among those around him. . . . Woe to the heart that has not loved in youth!

Thus Ivan Petrovitch found him, and without loss of time he set to work to apply his system to him.

'I want above all to make a man, *un homme*, of him,' he said to Glafira Petrovna, 'and not only a man, but a Spartan.' Ivan Petrovitch began carrying out his intentions by putting his son in a Scotch kilt; the twelve-year-old boy had to go about with bare knees and a plume stuck in his Scotch cap. The Swedish lady was replaced by a young Swiss tutor, who was versed in gymnastics to perfection. Music, as a pursuit unworthy of a man, was discarded. The natural sciences, international law, mathematics, carpentry, after Jean-Jacques Rousseau's precept, and heraldry, to encourage chivalrous feelings, were what the future 'man' was to be occupied with. He was waked at four o'clock in the morning, splashed at once with cold water and set to running round a high pole with a cord; he had only one meal a day, consisting of a single dish; rode on horseback; shot with a cross-bow; at every convenient opportunity he was exercised in acquiring after his parent's example firmness of will, and every evening he inscribed in a special book an account of the day and his impressions; and Ivan Petrovitch on his side wrote him instructions in French in which he called him *mon fils*, and addressed him as *vous*. In Russian Fedya called his father *thou*, but did not dare to sit down in his presence. The 'system' dazed the boy, confused and cramped his intellect, but his health on the other hand was benefited by the new manner of life; at first he fell into a fever but soon recovered and began to grow stout and strong. His father was proud of him and called him in his strange jargon 'a child of nature, my creation'. When Fedya had reached his sixteenth year, Ivan Petrovitch thought it his duty in good time to instil into him a contempt for the female sex; and the young Spartan, with timidity in his heart and the first down on his lip, full of sap and strength and young blood, already tried to seem indifferent, cold, and rude.

Meanwhile time was passing. Ivan Petrovitch spent the greater part of the year in Lavriky (that was the name of the principal estate inherited from his ancestors). But in the winter he used to go to Moscow alone; there he stayed at a tavern, diligently visited the club, made speeches and developed his plans in drawing-rooms, and in his behaviour was more than ever Anglomaniac, grumbling and political. But the year 1825 came and brought much sorrow. Intimate friends and acquaintances of Ivan Petrovitch underwent painful experiences. Ivan Petrovitch made haste to withdraw into the country and shut himself up in his house. Another year passed by, and suddenly Ivan Petrovitch grew feeble, and ailing; his health began to break up. He, the free-thinker, began to go to church and have prayers put up for him; he, the European, began to sit in steam-baths, to dine at two o'clock, to go to bed at nine, and to doze off to the sound of the chatter of the old steward; he, the man of political ideas, burnt all his schemes, all his correspondence, trembled before the governor, and was uneasy at the sight of the police-captain; he, the man of iron will, whimpered and complained, when he had a gumboil or when they gave him a plate of cold soup. Glafira Petrovna again took control of everything in the house; once more the overseers, bailiffs and simple peasants began to come to the back stairs to speak to the 'old witch', as the servants called her. The change in Ivan Petrovitch produced a powerful impression on his son. He had now reached his nineteenth year, and had begun to reflect and to emancipate himself from the hand that pressed like a weight upon him. Even before this time he had observed a little discrepancy between his father's words and deeds, between his wide liberal theories and his harsh petty despotism; but he had not expected such a complete breakdown. His confirmed egoism was patent now in everything. Young Lavretsky was getting ready to go to Moscow, to prepare for the university, when a new unexpected calamity overtook Ivan Petrovitch; he became blind, and hopelessly blind, in one day.

Having no confidence in the skill of Russian doctors, he began to make efforts to obtain permission to go abroad. It was refused. Then he took his son with him and for three whole years was wandering about Russia, from one doctor to another, incessantly moving from one town to another, and driving his physicians, his son, and his servants to despair by his cowardice and impatience. He returned to Lavriky a perfect wreck, a tearful and capricious child. Bitter days followed, everyone had much to put up with from him. Ivan Petrovitch was only quiet when he was dining; he had never been so greedy and eaten so much; all the rest of the time he gave himself and others no peace. He prayed, cursed his fate, abused himself, abused politics, his system, abused everything he had boasted of and prided himself upon, everything he had held up to his son as a model; he declared that he believed in nothing and then began to pray again; he could not put up with one instant of solitude, and expected his household to sit by his chair continually day and night, and entertain him with stories, which he constantly interrupted with exclamations, 'You are for ever lying, . . . a pack of nonsense!'

Glafira Petrovna was specially necessary to him; he absolutely could not get on without her—and to the end she always carried out every whim of the sick man, though sometimes she could not bring herself to answer at once, for fear the sound of her voice should betray her inward anger. Thus he lingered on for two years and died on the first day of May, when he had been brought out on to the balcony into the sun. 'Glasha, Glashka! soup, soup, old foo'—— his halting tongue muttered and before he had articulated the last word, it was silent for ever. Glafira Petrovna, who had only just taken the cup of soup from the hands of the steward, stopped, looked at her brother's face, slowly made a large sign of the cross and turned away in silence; and his son, who happened to be there, also said nothing; he leaned on the railing of the balcony and gazed a long while into the garden, all fragrant and green, and shining in the rays of the golden sunshine of spring. He was twenty-three years old; how terribly, how imperceptibly quickly those twenty-three years had passed by! . . . Life was opening before him.

✳ *12* ✳

After burying his father and entrusting to the unchanged Glafira Petrovna the management of his estate and superintendence of his bailiffs, young Lavretsky went to Moscow, whither he felt drawn by a vague but strong attraction. He recognised the defects of his education, and formed the resolution, as far as possible, to regain lost ground. In the last five years he had read much and seen something; he had many stray ideas in his head; any professor might have envied some of his acquirements, but at the same time he did not know much that every schoolboy would have learnt long ago. Lavretsky was aware of his limitations; he was secretly conscious of being eccentric. The Anglomaniac had done his son an ill turn; his whimsical education had produced its fruits. For long years he had submitted unquestioningly to his father; when at last he began to see through him, the evil was already done, his habits were deeply-rooted. He could not get on with people; at twenty-three years old, with an unquenchable thirst for love in his shy heart, he had never yet dared to look one woman in the face. With his intellect, clear and sound, but somewhat heavy, with his tendencies to obstinacy, contemplation, and indolence he ought from his earliest years to have been thrown into the stream of life, and he had been kept instead in artificial seclusion. And now the magic circle was broken, but he continued to remain within it, prisoned and pent up within himself. It was ridiculous at his age to put on a student's dress, but he was not afraid of ridicule; his Spartan education had at least the good effect of developing in him a contempt for the opinion of others, and he put on, without embarrassment, the academical uniform. He entered the section of physics and mathematics. Robust, rosy-cheeked, bearded, and taciturn, he produced a strange impression on his companions; they did not suspect that this austere man, who came so punctually to the lectures in a wide village sledge with a pair of horses, was inwardly almost a child. He appeared to them to be a queer kind of pedant; they did not care for him, and made no overtures to him, and he avoided them. During the first two years he spent in the university, he only made acquaintance with one student, from whom he took lessons in Latin. This student Mihalevitch by name, an enthusiast and a poet, who loved Lavretsky sincerely, by chance became the means of bringing about an important change in his destiny.

One day at the theatre—Motchalov was then at the height of his fame and Lavretsky did not miss a single performance—he saw in a box in the front tier a young girl, and though no woman ever came near his grim figure without setting his heart beating, it had never beaten so violently before. The young girl sat motionless, leaning with her elbows on the velvet of the box; the light of youth and life played in every feature of her dark, oval, lovely face; subtle intelligence was expressed in the splendid eyes which gazed softly and attentively from under her fine brows, in the swift smile on her expressive lips, in the very pose of her head, her hands, her neck. She was exquisitely dressed. Beside her sat a yellow and wrinkled woman of forty-five, with a low neck, in a black headdress, with a toothless smile on her intently-preoccupied and empty face, and in the inner recesses of the box was visible an edlerly man in a wide frock-coat and high cravat, with an expression of dull dignity and a kind of ingratiating distrustfulness in his little eyes, with dyed moustache and whiskers, a large meaningless forehead and wrinkled cheeks, by every sign a retired general. Lavretsky did not take his eyes off the girl who had made such an impression on him; suddenly the door of the box opened and Mihalevitch went in. The appearance of this man, almost his one acquaintance in Moscow, in the society of the one girl who was absorbing his whole attention, struck him as curious and significant. Continuing to gaze into the box, he observed that all the persons in it treated Mihalevitch as an old friend. The performance on the stage ceased to interest Lavretsky, even Motchalov though he was that evening in his 'best form', did not produce the usual impression on him. At one very pathetic part, Lavretsky involuntarily looked at his beauty: she was bending forward, her cheeks glowing, under the influence of his persistent gaze, her eyes, which were fixed on the stage, slowly turned and rested on him. All night he was haunted by those eyes. The skilfully constructed barriers were broken down at last; he was in a shiver and a fever, and the next day he went to Mihalevitch. From him he learnt that the name of the beauty was Varvara Pavlovna Korobyin; that the old people sitting with her in the box were her father and mother; and that he, Mihalevitch, had become acquainted with them a year before, while he was staying at Count N.'s, in the position of a tutor, near Moscow. The enthusiast spoke in rapturous praise of Varvara Pavlovna. 'My dear fellow,' he exclaimed with the impetuous ring in his voice peculiar to him, 'that girl is a marvellous creature, a genius, an artist in the true sense of the word, and she is very good too.' Noticing from Lavretsky's inquiries the impression Varvara Pavlovna had made on him, he himself proposed to introduce him to her, adding that he was like one of the family with them; that the general was not at all proud, and the mother was so stupid she could not say 'Bo' to a goose. Lavretsky blushed, muttered something unintelligible, and ran away. For five whole days he was struggling with his timidity; on the sixth day the young Spartan got into a new uniform and placed himself at Mihalevitch's disposal. The latter being his own valet, confined himself to combing his hair—and both betook themselves to the Korobyins.

* *13* *

Varvara Pavlovna's father, Pavel Petrovitch Korobyin, a retired general-major, had spent his whole time on duty in Petersburg. He had had the reputation in his youth of a good dancer and driller. Through poverty, he had served as adjutant to two or three generals of no distinction, and had married the daughter of one of them with a dowry of twenty-five thousand roubles. He mastered all the science of military discipline and manoeuvres to the minutest niceties, he went on in harness, till at last, after twenty-five years' service, he received the rank of a general and the command of a regiment. Then he might have relaxed his efforts and have quietly secured his pecuniary position. Indeed this was what he reckoned upon doing, but he managed things a little incautiously. He devised a new method of speculating with public funds—the method seemed an excellent one in itself—but he neglected to bribe in the right place, and was consequently informed against, and a more than unpleasant, a disgraceful scandal followed. The general got out of the affair somehow, but his career was ruined; he was advised to retire from active duty. For two years he lingered on in Petersburg, hoping to drop into some snug berth in the civil service, but no such snug berth came in his way. His daughter had left school, his expenses were increasing every day. Resigning himself to his fate, he decided to remove to Moscow for the sake of the greater cheapness of living, and took a tiny low-pitched house in the Old Stables Road, with a coat of arms seven feet long on the roof, and there began the life of a retired general at Moscow on an income of 2,750 roubles a year. Moscow is a hospitable city, ready to welcome all stray comers, generals by preference. Pavel Petrovitch's heavy figure, which was not quite devoid of martial dignity, however, soon began to be seen in the best drawing-rooms in Moscow. His bald head with its tufts of dyed hair, and the soiled ribbon of the Order of St Anne which he wore over a cravat of the colour of a raven's wing, began to be familiar to all the pale and listless young men who hang morosely about the card-tables while dancing is going on. Pavel Petrovitch knew how to gain a footing in society; he spoke little, but, from old habit, condescendingly—though, of course, not when he was talking to persons of a higher rank than his own. He played cards carefully; ate moderately at home, but consumed enough for six at parties. Of his wife there is scarcely anything to be said. Her name was Kalliopa Karlovna. There was always a tear in her left eye, on the strength of which Kalliopa Karlovna (she was, one must add, of German extraction) considered herself a woman of great sensibility. She was always in a state of nervous agitation, seemed as though she were ill-nourished, and wore a tight velvet dress, a cap, and tarnished hollow bracelets. The only daughter of Pavel Petrovitch and Kalliopa Karlovna, Varvara Pavlovna, was only just seventeen when she left the boarding-school, in which she had been reckoned, if not the prettiest, at least the cleverest pupil and the best musician, and where she had taken a decoration. She was not yet nineteen, when Lavretsky saw her for the first time.

14

The young Spartan's legs shook under him when Mihalevitch conducted him into the rather shabbily furnished drawing-room of the Korobyins, and presented him to them. But his overwhelming feeling of timidity soon disappeared. In the general the good-nature innate in all Russians was intensified by that special kind of geniality which is peculiar to all people who have done something disgraceful, the general's lady was as it were overlooked by everyone; and as for Varvara Pavlovna, she was so self-possessed and easily cordial that everyone at once felt at home in her presence; besides, about all her fascinating person, her smiling eyes, her faultlessly sloping shoulders and rosy-tinged white hands, her light and yet languid movements, the very sound of her voice, slow and sweet, there was an impalpable, subtle charm, like a faint perfume, voluptuous, tender, soft, though still modest, something which is hard to translate into words, but which moved and kindled—and timidity was not the feeling it kindled. Lavretsky turned the conversation on the theatre, on the performance of the previous day; she at once began herself to discuss Motchalov, and did not confine herself to sighs and interjections only, but uttered a few true observations full of feminine insight in regard to his acting. Mihalevitch spoke about music; she sat down without ceremony to the piano, and very correctly played some of Chopin's mazurkas, which were then just coming into fashion. Dinner-time came; Lavretsky would have gone away, but they made him stay: at dinner the general regaled him with excellent Lafitte, which the general's lackey hurried off in a street-sledge to Dupré's to fetch. Late in the evening Lavretsky returned home; for a long while he sat without undressing, covering his eyes with his hands in the stupefaction of enchantment. It seemed to him that now for the first time he understood what made life worth living; all his previous assumptions, all his plans, all that rubbish and nonsense had vanished into nothing at once; all his soul was absorbed in one feeling, in one desire—in the desire of happiness, of possession, of love, the sweet love of a woman. From that day he began to go often to the Korobyins.

Six months later he spoke to Varvara Pavlovna, and offered her his hand. His offer was accepted; the general had long before, almost on the eve of Lavretsky's first visit, inquired of Mihalevitch how many serfs Lavretsky owned; and indeed Varvara Pavlovna, who through the whole time of the young man's courtship, and even at the very moment of his declaration, had preserved her customary composure and clearness of mind—Varvara Pavlovna too was very well aware that her suitor was a wealthy man; and Kalliopa Karlovna thought '*meine Tochter macht eine schöne Partie,*' and bought herself a new cap.

* *15* *

And so his offer was accepted, but on certain conditions. In the first place, Lavretsky was at once to leave the university; who would be married to a student, and what a strange idea too—how could a landowner, a rich man, at twenty-six, take lessons and be at school? Secondly, Varvara Pavlovna took upon herself the labour of ordering and purchasing her trousseau, and even choosing her present from the bridegroom. She had much practical sense, a great deal of taste, and a very great love of comfort, together with a great faculty for obtaining it for herself. Lavretsky was especially struck by this faculty when, immediately after their wedding, he travelled alone with his wife in the comfortable carriage, bought by her, to Lavriky. How carefully everything with which he was surrounded had been thought of, devised and provided before-hand by Varvara Pavlovna! What charming travelling knick-knacks appeared from various snug corners, what fascinating toilet-cases and coffee-pots, and how delightfully Varvara Pavlovna herself made the coffee in the morning! Lavretsky, however, was not at that time disposed to be observant; he was blissful, drunk with happiness; he gave himself up to it like a child. Indeed he was as innocent as a child, this young Hercules. Not in vain was the whole personality of his young wife breathing with fascination; not in vain was her promise

to the senses of a mysterious luxury of untold bliss; her fulfilment was richer than her promise. When she reached Lavriky
in the very height of the summer, she found the house dark
and dirty, the servants absurd and old-fashioned, but she did
not think it necessary even to hint at this to her husband. If she
had proposed to establish herself at Lavriky, she would have
changed everything in it, beginning of course with the house;
but the idea of staying in that out-of-the-way corner of the
steppes never entered her head for an instant; she lived as in
a tent, good-temperedly putting up with all its inconveniences,
and indulgently making merry over them. Marfa Timofyevna
came to pay a visit to her former charge; Varvara Pavlovna
liked her very much, but she did not like Varvara Pavlovna.
The new mistress did not get on with Glafira Petrovna either;
she would have left her in peace, but old Korobyin wanted to
have a hand in the management of his son-in-law's affairs; to
superintend the property of such a near relative, he said, was
not beneath the dignity even of a general. One must add that
Pavel Petrovitch would not have been above managing the property even of a total stranger. Varvara Pavlovna conducted
her attack very skilfully, without taking any step in advance,
apparently completely absorbed in the bliss of the honeymoon,
in the peaceful life of the country, in music and reading, she
gradually worked Glafira up to such a point that she rushed
one morning, like one possessed, into Lavretsky's study, and
throwing a bunch of keys on the table, she declared that she
was not equal to undertaking the management any longer, and
did not want to stop in the place. Lavretsky, having been
suitably prepared beforehand, at once agreed to her departure.
This Glafira Petrovna had not anticipated. 'Very well,' she
said, and her face darkened, 'I see that I am not wanted here!
I know who is driving me out of the home of my fathers. Only
you mark my words, nephew; you will never make a home
anywhere, you will come to be a wanderer for ever. That is my
last word to you.' The same day she went away to her own
little property, and in a week General Korobyin was there,
and with a pleasant melancholy in his looks and movements
he took the superintendence of the whole property into his
hands.

In the month of September, Varvara Pavlovna carried her

husband off to Petersburg. She passed two winters in Petersburg (for the summer she went to stay at Tsarskoe Selo), in a splendid, light, artistically-furnished flat; they made many acquaintances among the middle and even higher ranks of society; went out and entertained a great deal, and gave the most charming dances and musical evenings. Varvara Pavlovna attracted guests as a fire attracts moths. Fedor Ivanitch did not altogether like such a frivolous life. His wife advised him to take some office under government; but from old association with his father, and also through his own ideas, he was unwilling to enter government service, still he remained in Petersburg for Varvara Pavlovna's pleasure. He soon discovered, however, that no one hindered him from being alone; that it was not for nothing that he had the quietest and most comfortable study in all Petersburg; that his tender wife was even ready to aid him to be alone; and from that time forth all went well. He again applied himself to his own, as he considered, unfinished education; he began again to read, and even began to learn English. It was a strange sight to see his powerful, broad-shouldered figure for ever bent over his writing table, his full-bearded ruddy face half buried in the pages of a dictionary or note-book. Every morning he set to work, then had a capital dinner (Varvara Pavlovna was unrivalled as a housekeeper), and in the evenings he entered an enchanted world of light and perfume, peopled by gay young faces, and the centre of this world was also the careful housekeeper, his wife. She rejoiced his heart by the birth of a son, but the poor child did not live long; it died in the spring, and in the summer, by the advice of the doctors, Lavretsky took his wife abroad to a watering-place. Distraction was essential for her after such a trouble, and her health, too, required a warm climate. The summer and autumn they spent in Germany and Switzerland, and for the winter, as one would naturally expect, they went to Paris. In Paris, Varvara Pavlovna bloomed like a rose, and was able to make herself a little nest as quickly and cleverly as in Petersburg. She found very pretty apartments in one of the quiet but fashionable streets in Paris; she embroidered her husband such a dressing-gown as he had never worn before; engaged a coquettish waiting maid, an excellent cook, and a smart footman, procured a fascinating carriage, and an exquisite piano. Before a week had passed, she crossed the street, wore her shawl, opened her parasol, and put on her gloves in a manner equal to the most true-born Parisian. And she soon drew round herself acquaintances. At first, only Russians visited her, afterwards Frenchmen too, very agreeable, polite, and unmarried, with excellent manners and well-sounding names; they all talked a great deal and very fast, bowed easily, grimaced agreeably; their white teeth flashed under their rosy lips—and how they could smile! All of them brought their friends, and *la belle Madame de Lavretsky* was soon known from Chaussée d'Antin to Rue de Lille. In those days—it was in 1836—there had not yet arisen the tribe of journalists and reporters who now swarm on all sides like ants in an ant-hill; but even then there was seen in Varvara Pavlovna's salon a certain M. Jules, a gentleman of unprepossessing exterior, with a scandalous reputation, insolent and mean, like all duellists and men who have been beaten. Varvara Pavlovna felt a great aversion to this M. Jules, but she received him because he wrote for various journals, and was incessantly mentioning her, calling her at one time *Madame de L . . . tzki*, at another, *Madame de . . . , cette grande dame russe si distinguée, qui demeure rue de P. . . .* and telling all the world, that is, some hundreds of readers who had nothing to do with Madame de L . . . tzki, how charming and delightful this lady was; a true Frenchwoman in intelligence (*une vraie française par l'esprit*)—Frenchmen have no higher praise than this—what an extraordinary musician she was, and how marvellously she waltzed (Varvara Pavlovna did in fact waltz so that she drew all her hearts to the hem of her light flying skirts)—in a word, he spread her fame through the world, and, whatever one may say, that is pleasant. Mademoiselle Mars had already left the stage, and Mademoiselle Rachel had not yet made her appearance; nevertheless, Varvara Pavlovna was assiduous in visiting the theatres. She went into raptures over Italian music, yawned decorously at the Comédie Française, and wept at the acting of Madame Dorval in some ultra-romantic melodrama; and a great thing—Liszt played twice in her salon, and was so kind, so simple—it was charming! In such agreeable sensations was spent the winter, at the end of which Varvara Pavlovna was even presented at court. Fedor Ivanitch, for his part, was not bored, though his life, at times, weighed rather heavily on him—because it was empty. He read the papers, listened to the lectures at the Sorbonne and the Collège de France, followed the debates in the Chambers, and set to work on a translation of a well-known scientific treatise on irrigation. 'I am not wasting my time,' he thought, 'it is all of use; but next winter I must, without fail, return to Russia and set to work.' It is difficult to say whether he had any clear idea of precisely what this work would consist of; and there is no telling whether he would have succeeded in going to Russia in the winter; in the meantime, he was going with his wife to Baden . . . An unexpected incident broke up all his plans.

* 16 *

Happening to go one day in Varvara Pavlovna's absence into her boudoir, Lavretsky saw on the floor a carefully folded little paper. He mechanically picked it up, unfolded it, and read the following note, written in French:

'Sweet angel Betsy! (I never can make up my mind to call you Barbe or Varvara), I waited in vain for you at the corner of the boulevard; come to our little room at half-past one to-morrow. Your stout good-natured husband (*ton gros bonhomme de mari*) is usually buried in his books at that time; we will sing once more the song of your poet *Pouskine* (*de votre poète Pouskine*) that you taught me: "Old husband, cruel husband!" A thousand kisses on your little hands and feet. I await you.'

'ERNEST.'

Lavretsky did not at once understand what he had read; he read it a second time, and his head began to swim, the ground began to sway under his feet like the deck of a ship in a rolling sea. He began to cry out and gasp and weep all at the same instant.

He was utterly overwhelmed. He had so blindly believed in his wife; the possibility of deception, of treason, had never presented itself to his mind. This Ernest, his wife's lover, was a fair-haired pretty boy of three-and-twenty, with a little turned-up nose and refined little moustaches, almost the most insignificant of all her acquaintances. A few minutes passed, half an hour passed, Lavretsky still stood, crushing the fatal note in his hands, and gazing senselessly at the floor; across a kind of tempest of darkness pale shapes hovered about him; his heart was numb with anguish; he seemed to be falling, falling—and a bottomless abyss was opening at his feet. A familiar light rustle of a silk dress roused him from his numbness; Varvara Pavlovna in her hat and shawl was returning in haste from her walk. Lavretsky trembled all over and rushed away; he felt that at that instant he was capable of tearing her to pieces, beating her to death, as a peasant might do, strangling her with his own hands. Varvara Pavlovna in amazement tried to stop him; he could only whisper, 'Betsy',—and ran out of the house.

Lavretsky took a cab and ordered the man to drive him out of the town. All the rest of the day and the whole night he wandered about, constantly stopping short and wringing his hands, at one moment he was mad, and the next he was ready to laugh, was even merry after a fashion. By the morning he grew calm through exhaustion, and went into a wretched tavern in the outskirts, asked for a room and sat down on a chair before the window. He was overtaken by a fit of convulsive yawning. He could scarcely stand upright, his whole body was worn out, and he did not even feel fatigue, though fatigue began to do its work; he sat and gazed and comprehended nothing; he did not understand what had happened to him, why he found himself alone, with his limbs stiff, with a taste of bitterness in his mouth, with a load on his heart, in an empty unfamiliar room; he did not understand what had impelled her, his Varya, to give herself to this Frenchman, and how, knowing herself unfaithful, she could go on being just as calm, just as affectionate, as confidential with him as before! 'I cannot understand it!' his parched lips whispered. 'Who can guarantee now that even in Petersburg' . . . And he did not finish the question, and yawned again, shivering and shaking all over. Memories—bright and gloomy—fretted him alike; suddenly it crossed his mind how some days before she had sat down to the piano and sung before him and Ernest the song, 'Old husband, cruel husband!' He recalled the expression of her face, the strange light in her eyes, and the colour on her cheeks—and he got up from his seat, he would have liked to go to them, to tell them: 'You were wrong to play your tricks on me; my great-grandfather used to hang the peasants up by their ribs, and my grandfather was himself a peasant,' and to kill them both. Then all at once it seemed to him as if all that was happening was a dream, scarcely even a dream, but some kind of foolish joke; that he need only shake himself and look round. . . . He looked round, and like a hawk clutching its captured prey, anguish gnawed deeper and deeper into his heart. To complete it all, Lavretsky had been hoping in a few months to be a father. . . . The past, the future, his whole life was poisoned. He went back at last to Paris, stopped at an hotel and sent M. Ernest's note to Varvara Pavlovna with the following letter:—

'The enclosed scrap of paper will explain everything to you. Let me tell you by the way, that I was surprised at you; you, who are always so careful, to leave such valuable papers lying about.' (Poor Lavretsky had spent hours preparing and gloating over this phrase.) 'I cannot see you again; I imagine that you, too, would hardly desire an interview with me. I am assigning you 15,000 francs a year; I cannot give more. Send your address to the office of the estate. Do what you please; live where you please. I wish you happiness. No answer is needed.'

Lavretsky wrote to his wife that he needed no answer . . . but he waited, he thirsted for a reply, for an explanation of this incredible, inconceivable thing. Varvara Pavlovna wrote him the same day a long letter in French. It put the finishing touch; his last doubts vanished,—and he began to feel ashamed that he had still had any doubt left. Varvara Pavlovna did not attempt to defend herself; her only desire was to see him, she besought him not to condemn her irrevocably. The letter was cold and constrained, though here and there traces of tears were visible. Lavretsky smiled bitterly, and sent word by the messenger that it was all right. Three days later he was no longer in Paris; but he did not go to Russia, but to Italy. He did not know himself why he fixed upon Italy; he did not really care where he went—so long as it was not home. He sent instructions to his steward on the subject of his wife's allowance, and at the same time told him to take all control of his property out of General Korobyin's hands at once, without waiting for him to draw up an account, and to make arrangements for his Excellency's departure from Lavriky; he could picture vividly the confusion, the vain airs of self-importance of the dispossessed general, and in the midst of all his sorrow, he felt a kind of spiteful satisfaction. At the same time he asked Glafira Petrovna by letter to return to Lavriky, and drew up a deed authorising her to take possession; Glafira Petrovna did not return to Lavriky, and printed in the newspapers that the deed was cancelled, which was perfectly unnecessary on her part. Lavretsky kept out of sight in a small Italian town, but for a long time he could not help following his wife's movements. From the newspapers he learned that she had gone from Paris to Baden as she had arranged; her name soon appeared in an article written by the same M. Jules. In this article there was a kind of sympathetic condolence apparent under the habitual playfulness; there was a deep sense of disgust in the soul of Fedor Ivanitch as he read this article. Afterwards he learned that a daughter had been born to him; two months later he received a notification from his steward that Varvara Pavlovna had asked for the first quarter's allowance. Then worse and worse rumours began to reach him; at last, a tragic-comic story was reported with acclamations in all the papers. His wife played an unenviable part in it. It was the finishing stroke; Varvara Pavlovna had become a 'notoriety'.

Lavretsky ceased to follow her movements; but he could not quickly gain mastery over himself. Sometimes he was overcome by such a longing for his wife that he would have given up everything, he thought, even, perhaps . . . could have forgiven her, only to hear her caressing voice again, to feel again her hand in his. Time, however, did not pass in vain. He was not born to be a victim; his healthy nature reasserted its rights. Much became clear to him; even the blow that had fallen on him no longer seemed to him to have been quite un-

foreseen; he understood his wife,—we can only fully understand those who are near to us, when we are separated
from them. He could take up his interests, could work again,
though with nothing like his former zeal; scepticism, half-
formed already by the experiences of his life, and by his
education, took complete possession of his heart. He became
indifferent to everything. Four years passed by, and he felt
himself strong enough to return to his country, to meet his
own people. Without stopping at Petersburg or at Moscow
he came to the town of O——, where we parted from him,
and whither we will now ask the indulgent reader to return
with us.

* 17 *

The morning after the day we have described, at ten o'clock,
Lavretsky was mounting the steps of the Kalitins' house. He
was met by Lisa coming out in her hat and gloves.
'Where are you going?' he asked her.
'To service. It is Sunday.'
'Why, do you go to church?'
Lisa looked at him in silent amazement.
'I beg your pardon,' said Lavretsky; 'I—I did not mean to
say that; I have come to say good-bye to you, I am starting
for my village in an hour.'
'Is it far from here?' asked Lisa.
'Twenty miles.'
Lenotchka made her appearance in the doorway, escorted
by a maid.
'Mind you don't forget us,' observed Lisa, and went down
the steps.
'And don't you forget me. And listen,' he added, 'you are
going to church; while you are there, pray for me too.'
Lisa stopped short and turned round to him: 'Certainly,'
she said, looking him straight in the face, 'I will pray for you
too. Come, Lenotchka.'
In the drawing-room Lavretsky found Marya Dmitrievna
alone. She was redolent of *eau de Cologne* and mint. She had,

as she said, a headache, and had passed a restless night. She received him with her usual languid graciousness and gradually fell into conversation.

'Vladimir Nikolaitch is really a delightful young man, don't you think so?' she asked him.

'What Vladimir Nikolaitch?'

'Panshin to be sure, who was here yesterday. He took a tremendous fancy to you; I will tell you a secret, *mon cher cousin*, he is simply crazy about my Lisa. Well, he is of good family, has a capital position in the service, and a clever fellow, a kammer-yunker, and if it is God's will, I for my part, as a mother, shall be well pleased. My responsibility of course is immense; the happiness of children depends, no doubt, on parents; still I may say, up till now, for better or for worse I have done everything, I alone have been everywhere with them, that is to say, I have educated my children and taught them everything myself. Now, indeed, I have written for a French governess from Madame Boluce.'

Marya Dmitrievna launched into a description of her cares and anxieties and maternal sentiments. Lavretsky listened in silence, turning his hat in his hands. His cold, weary glance embarrassed the gossiping lady.

'And do you like Lisa?' she asked.

'Lisaveta Mihalovna is an excellent girl,' replied Lavretsky, and he got up, took his leave, and went off to Marfa Timofyevna. Marya Dmitrievna looked after him in high displeasure, and thought, 'What a dolt, a regular peasant! Well, now I understand why his wife could not remain faithful to him.'

Marfa Timofyevna was sitting in her room, surrounded by her little court. It consisted of five creatures almost equally near her heart; a big-cropped, learned bullfinch, which she had taken a fancy to because he had lost his accomplishments of whistling and drawing water; a very timid and peaceable little dog, Roska; an ill-tempered cat, Matross; a dark-faced, agile little girl of nine years old, with big eyes and a sharp nose, called Shurotchka; and an elderly woman of fifty-five, in a white cap and a cinnamon-coloured abbreviated jacket, over a dark skirt, by name, Nastasya Karpovna Ogarkov. Shurotchka was an orphan of the tradesman class. Marfa

Timofyevna had taken her to her heart like Roska, from compassion; she had found the little dog and the little girl too in the street; both were thin and hungry, both were being drenched by the autumn rain; no one came in search of Roska, and Shurotchka was given up to Marfa Timofyevna with positive eagerness by her uncle, a drunken shoemaker, who did not get enough to eat himself, and did not feed his niece, but beat her over the head with his last. With Nastasya Karpovna Marfa Timofyevna had made acquaintance on a pilgrimage at a monastery; she had gone up to her at the church (Marfa Timofyevna took a fancy to her because in her own words she said her prayers so prettily) and had addressed her and invited her to a cup of tea. From that day she never parted from her. Nastasya Karpovna was a woman of the most cheerful and gentle disposition, a widow without children, of poor noble family; she had a round grey head, soft white hands, a soft face with large mild features, and a rather absurd turned-up nose; she stood in awe of Marfa Timofyevna, and the latter was very fond of her, though she laughed at her susceptibility. She had a soft place in her heart for every young man, and could not help blushing like a girl at the most innocent joke. Her whole fortune consisted of only 1,200 roubles; she lived at Marfa Timofyevna's expense, but on an equal footing with her: Marfa Timofyevna would not have put up with any servility.

'Ah! Fedya,' she began, directly she saw him, 'last night you did not see my family, you must admire them, we are all here together for tea; this is our second, holiday tea. You can make friends with them all; only Shurotchka won't let you, and the cat will scratch. Are you starting to-day?'

'Yes.' Lavretsky sat down on a low seat, 'I have just said good-bye to Marya Dmitrievna. I saw Lisaveta Mihalovna too.'

'Call her Lisa, my dear fellow. Mihalovna indeed to you! But sit still, or you will break Shurotchka's little chair.'

'She has gone to church,' continued Lavretsky. 'Is she religious?'

'Yes, Fedya, very much so. More than you and I, Fedya.'

'Aren't you religious then?' lisped Nastasya Karpovna. 'To-day, you have not been to the early service, but you are going to the late.'

'No, not at all; you will go alone; I have grown too lazy, my dear,' replied Marfa Timofyevna. 'Already I am indulging myself with tea.' She addressed Nastasya Karpovna in the singular, though she treated her as an equal. She was not a Pestov for nothing: three Pestovs had been on the death-list of Ivan the Terrible, Marfa Timofyevna was well aware of the fact.

'Tell me, please,' began Lavretsky again, 'Marya Dmitrievna has just been talking to me about this—what's his name? Panshin. What sort of a man is he?'

'What a chatterbox she is, Lord save us!' muttered Marfa Timofyevna. 'She told you, I suppose, as a secret that he has turned up as a suitor. She might have whispered it to her priest's son; no, he's not enough for her, it seems. And so far there's nothing to tell, thank God, but already she's gossiping about it.'

'Why thank God?' asked Lavretsky.

'Because I don't like the fine young gentleman; and so what is there to be glad of in it?'

'You don't like him?'

'No, he can't fascinate everyone. He must be satisfied with Nastasya Karpovna's being in love with him.'

The poor widow was utterly dismayed.

'How can you, Marfa Timofyevna? you've no conscience!' she cried, and a crimson flush instantly overspread her face and neck.

'And he knows, to be sure, the rogue,' Marfa Timofyevna interrupted her, 'he knows how to captivate her; he made her a present of a snuff-box. Fedya, ask her for a pinch of snuff; you will see what a splendid snuff-box it is; on the lid a hussar on horseback. You'd better not try to defend yourself, my dear.'

Nastasya Karpovna could only fling up her hands.

'Well, but Lisa,' inquired Lavretsky, 'is she indifferent to him?'

'She seems to like him, but there, God knows! The heart of another, you know, is a dark forest, and a girl's more than any. Shurotchka's heart, for instance—I defy you to understand it! What makes her hide herself and not come out ever since you came in?'

Shurotchka choked with suppressed laughter and skipped out of the room. Lavretsky rose from his place.

'Yes,' he said in an uncertain voice, 'there is no deciphering a girl's heart.'

He began to say good-bye.

'Well, shall we see you again soon?' inquired Marfa Timofyevna.

'Very likely, aunt: it's not far off, you know.'

'Yes, to be sure you are going to Vassilyevskoe. You don't care to stay at Lavriky: well, that's your own affair, only mind you go and say a prayer at your mother's grave, and your grandmother's too while you are there. Out there in foreign parts you have picked up all kinds of ideas, but who knows? Perhaps even in their graves they will feel that you have come to them. And, Fedya, don't forget to have a service sung too for Glafira Petrovna; here's a silver rouble for you. Take it, take it, I want to pay for a service for her. I had no love for her in her lifetime, but all the same there's no denying she was a girl of character. She was a clever creature; and a good friend to you. And now go and God be with you, before I weary you.'

And Marfa Timofyevna embraced her nephew.

'And Lisa's not going to marry Panshin; don't you trouble yourself; that's not the sort of husband she deserves.'

'Oh, I'm not troubling myself,' answered Lavretsky, and went away.

* 18 *

Four days later, he set off for home. His coach rolled quickly along the soft cross-road. There had been no rain for a fortnight; a fine milky mist was diffused in the air and hung over the distant woods; a smell of burning came from it. A multitude of darkish clouds with blurred edges were creeping across the pale blue sky; a fairly strong breeze blew a dry and steady gale, without dispelling the heat. Leaning back with his head on the cushion and his arms crossed on his breast, Lavretsky watched the furrowed fields unfolding like a fan before him, the willow bushes as they slowly came into sight, and the dull ravens and rooks, who looked sidelong with stupid suspicion at the approaching carriage, the long ditches, overgrown with mugwort, wormwood, and mountain ash; and as he watched the fresh fertile wilderness and solitude of this steppe country, the greenness, the long slopes, and valleys with stunted oak bushes, the grey villages, and scant birch-trees,—the whole Russian landscape, so long unseen by him, stirred emotion at once pleasant, sweet and almost painful in his heart, and he felt weighed down by a kind of pleasant oppression. Slowly his thoughts wandered; their outlines were as vague and indistinct as the outlines of the clouds which seemed to be wandering at random overhead. He remembered his childhood, his mother; he remembered her death, how they had carried him in to her, and how, clasping his head to her bosom, she had begun to wail over him, then had glanced at Glafira Petrovna—and checked herself. He remembered his father, at first vigorous, discontented with everything, with strident voice; and later, blind, tearful, with unkempt grey beard; he remembered how one day after drinking a glass too much at dinner, and spilling the gravy over his napkin, he began to relate his conquests, growing red in the face, and winking with his sightless eyes; he remembered Varvara Pavlovna,—and involuntarily shuddered, as a man shudders from a sudden internal pain, and shook his head. Then his thoughts came to a stop at Lisa.

'There,' he thought, 'is a new creature, only just entering on life. A nice girl, what will become of her? She is good-looking too. A pale, fresh face, mouth and eyes so serious, and an honest innocent expression. It is a pity she seems a little enthusiastic. A good figure, and she moves so lightly, and a soft voice. I like the way she stops suddenly, listens attentively, without a smile, then grows thoughtful and shakes back her hair. I fancy, too, that Panshin is not good enough for her. What's amiss with him, though? And besides, what business have I to wonder about it? She will go along the same road as all the rest. I had better go to sleep.' And Lavretsky closed his eyes.

He could not sleep, but he sank into the drowsy numbness of a journey. Images of the past rose slowly as before, floated in his soul, mixed and tangled up with other fancies. Lavretsky, for some unknown reason, began to think about Robert Peel, . . . about French history—of how he would gain a battle, if he were a general; he fancied the shots and the cries. . . . His head slipped on one side, he opened his eyes. The same fields, the same steppe scenery; the polished shoes of the trace-horses flashed alternately through the driving dust; the coachman's shirt, yellow with red gussets, was puffed out by the wind. . . . 'A nice home-coming!' glanced through Lavretsky's brain; and he cried, 'Get on!' wrapped himself in his cloak and pressed close into the cushion. The carriage jolted; Lavretsky sat up and opened his eyes wide. On the slope before him stretched a small hamlet; a little to the right could be seen an ancient manor-house of small size, with closed shutters and a winding flight of steps; nettles, green and thick as hemp, grew over the wide courtyard from the very gates; in it stood a store-house built of oak, still strong. This was Vassilyevskoe.

The coachman drove to the gates and drew up; Lavretsky's groom stood up on the box and as though in preparation for jumping down, shouted, 'Hey!' There was a sleepy, muffled sound of barking, but not even a dog made its appearance; the groom again made ready for a jump, and again shouted 'Hey!' The feeble barking was repeated, and an instant after a man from some unseen quarter ran into the courtyard, dressed in a nankeen coat, his head as white as snow; he stared at the coach, shading his eyes from the sun; all at once he slapped his thighs with both hands, ran to and fro a little, then rushed to open the gates. The coach drove into the yard, crushing the nettles with the wheels and drew up at the steps. The white-headed man, who seemed very alert, was already standing on the bottom step, his legs bent and wide apart. He unfastened the apron of the carriage, holding back the strap with a jerk and aiding his master to alight; then kissed his hand.

'How do you do, how do you do, brother?' began Lavretsky. 'Your name's Anton, I think? You are still alive, then?' The old man bowed without speaking, and ran off for the keys. While he went, the coachman sat motionless, sitting sideways and staring at the closed door, but Lavretsky's groom stood as he had leaped down in a picturesque pose with one arm thrown back on the box. The old man brought the keys, and, quite needlessly, twisting about like a snake, with his elbows raised high, he opened the door, stood on one side, and again bowed to the earth.

'So here I am at home, here I am back again,' thought Lavretsky, as he walked into the diminutive passage, while one after another the shutters were being opened with much creaking and knocking, and the light of day poured into the deserted rooms.

* *19* *

The small manor-house to which Lavretsky had come and in which two years before Glafira Petrovna had breathed her last, had been built in the preceding century of solid pine-wood; it looked ancient, but it was still strong enough to stand another fifty years or more. Lavretsky made the tour of all the rooms, and to the great discomfiture of the aged languid flies, settled under the lintels and covered with white dust, he ordered the windows to be opened everywhere; they had not been opened ever since the death of Glafira Petrovna. Everything in the house had remained as it was; the thin-legged white miniature couches in the drawing-room, covered with glossy grey stuff, threadbare and rickety, vividly suggested the days of Catherine; in the drawing-room, too, stood the mistress's favourite arm-chair, with high straight back, against which she never leaned even in her old age. On the principal wall hung a very old portrait of Fedor's great-grandfather, Andrey Lavretsky; the dark yellow face was scarcely distinguishable from the warped and blackened background; the small cruel eyes looked grimly out from beneath the eyelids, which drooped as if they were swollen; his black unpowdered hair rose bristling above his heavy indented brow. In the corner of the portrait hung a wreath of dusty immortelles. 'Glafira Petrovna herself was pleased to make it,' Anton announced. In the bedroom stood a narrow bed-stead, under a canopy of old-fashioned and very good striped material; a heap of faded cushions and a thin quilted counterpane lay on the bed, and at the head hung a picture of the Presentation in the Temple of the Holy Mother of God; it was the very picture which the old maid, dying alone and forgotten by everyone, had for the last time pressed to her chilling lips. A little toilet table of inlaid wood, with brass fittings and a warped looking-glass in a tarnished frame stood in the window. Next to the bedroom was the little ikon room with bare walls and a heavy case of holy images in the corner; on the floor lay a threadbare rug spotted with wax; Glafira Petrovna used to pray bowing to the ground upon it. Anton went away with Lavretsky's groom to unlock the stable and coach-house; to replace him appeared an old woman of about the same age, with a handkerchief tied round to her very eyebrows; her head shook, and her eyes were dim, but they expressed zeal, the habit of years of submissive service, and at the same time a kind of respectful commiseration. She kissed Lavretsky's hand and stood still in the doorway await-ing his orders. He positively could not recollect her name and did not even remember whether he had ever seen her. Her name, it appeared, was Apraxya; forty years before, Glafira Petrovna had put her out of the master's house and ordered that she should be poultry-woman. She said little, however; she seemed to have lost her senses from old age, and could only gaze at him obsequiously. Besides these two old crea-tures and three pot-bellied children in long smocks, Anton's great-grandchildren, there was also living in the manor-house a one-armed peasant, who was exempted from servitude; he muttered like a woodcock and was of no use for anything. Not much more useful was the decrepit dog who had saluted Lavretsky's return by its barking; he had been for ten years fastened up by a heavy chain, purchased at Glafira Petrovna's command, and was scarcely able to move and drag the weight of it. Having looked over the house, Lavretsky went into the garden and was very much pleased with it. It was all over-grown with high grass, and burdock, and gooseberry and raspberry bushes, but there was plenty of shade, and many old lime-trees, which were remarkable for their immense size and the peculiar growth of their branches; they had been planted too close and at some time or other—a hundred years before —they had been lopped. At the end of the garden was a small clear pool bordered with high reddish rushes. The traces of human life very quickly pass away; Glafira Petrovna's estate had not had time to become quite wild, but already it seemed plunged in that quiet slumber in which everything reposes on earth where there is not the infection of man's restlessness. Fedor Ivanitch walked also through the village; the peasant-women stared at him from the doorways of their huts, their cheeks resting on their hands; the peasants saluted him from a distance, the children ran out, and the dogs barked indiffer-ently. At last he began to feel hungry; but he did not expect his servants and his cook till the evening; the waggons of provisions from Lavriky had not come yet, and he had to have recourse to Anton. Anton arranged matters at once; he caught, killed, and plucked an old hen; Apraxya gave it a long rubbing and cleaning, and washed it like linen before putting it into the stew-pan; when, at last, it was cooked, Anton laid the cloth and set the table, placing beside the knife and fork a three-legged salt-cellar of tarnished plate and a cut decanter with a round glass stopper and a narrow neck; then he announced to Lavretsky in a sing-song voice that the meal was ready, and took his stand behind his chair, with a napkin twisted round his right fist, and diffusing about him a peculiar strong ancient odour, like the scent of a cypress-tree. Lavret-sky tried the soup, and took out the hen; its skin was all covered with large blisters; a tough tendon ran up each leg; the meat had a flavour of wood and soda. When he had finished dinner, Lavretsky said that he would drink a cup of tea, if——'I will bring it this minute,' the old man inter-rupted. And he kept his word. A pinch of tea was hunted up, twisted in a screw of red paper; a small but very fiery and loudly-hissing samovar was found, and sugar too in small lumps, which looked as if they were thawing. Lavretsky drank tea out of a large cup; he remembered this cup from childhood; there were playing-cards depicted upon it, only visitors used to drink out of it—and here was he drinking out of it like a visitor. In the evening his servants came; Lavretsky did not care to sleep in his aunt's bed; he directed them to put him up a bed in the dining-room. After extinguishing his candle he stared for a long time about him and fell into cheer-less reflection; he experienced that feeling which every man

knows whose lot it is to pass the night in a place long unin-
habited; it seemed to him that the darkness surrounding him
on all sides could not be accustomed to the new inhabitant,
the very walls of the house seemed amazed. At last he sighed,
drew up the counterpane round him and fell asleep. Anton
remained up after all the rest of the household; he was whis-
pering a long while with Apraxya, he sighed in an undertone,
and twice he crossed himself; they had neither of them expected that their master would settle among them at Vassilyevskoe when he had not far off such a splendid estate with such
a capitally built house; they did not suspect that the very
house was hateful to Lavretsky; it stirred painful memories
within him. Having gossiped to his heart's content, Anton
took a stick and struck the night watchman's board, which had
hung silent for so many years, and laid down to sleep in the
courtyard with no covering on his white head. The May night
was mild and soft, and the old man slept sweetly.

* 20 *

The next day Lavretsky got up rather early, had a talk with
the village bailiff, visited the threshing-floor, ordered the
chain to be taken off the yard dog, who only barked a little,
but did not even come out of his kennel, and, returning home,
sank into a kind of peaceful torpor, which he did not shake off
the whole day.

'Here I am at the very bottom of the river,' he said to himself more than once. He sat at the window without stirring,
and, as it were, listened to the current of the quiet life surrounding him, to the few sounds of the country solitude.
Something from behind the nettles chirps with a shrill, shrill
little note; a gnat seems to answer it. Now it has ceased, but
still the gnat keeps up its sharp whirr; across the pleasant,
persistent, fretful buzz of the flies sounds the hum of a big bee,
constantly knocking its head against the ceiling; a cock crows
in the street, hoarsely prolonging the last note; there is the
rattle of a cart; in the village a gate is creaking. Then the

jarring voice of a peasant woman, 'What?' 'Hey, you are my little sweetheart,' cries Anton to the little two-year-old girl he is dandling in his arms. 'Fetch the *kvas*,' repeats the same woman's voice, and all at once there follows a deathly silence; nothing rattles, nothing is moving; the wind is not stirring a leaf; without a sound the swallows fly one after another over the earth, and sadness weighs on the heart from their noiseless flight. 'Here I am at the very bottom of the river,' thought Lavretsky again. 'And always, at all times life here is quiet, unhasting,' he thought; 'whoever comes within its circle must submit; here there is nothing to agitate, nothing to harass; one can only get on here by making one's way slowly, as the ploughman cuts the furrow with his plough. And what vigour, what health abound in this inactive place! Here under the window the sturdy burdock creeps out of the thick grass; above it the lovage trails its juicy stalks, and the Virgin's tears fling still higher their pink tendrils; and yonder further in the fields is the silky rye, and the oats are already in ear, and every leaf on every tree, every grass on its stalk is spread to its fullest width. In the love of a woman my best years have gone by,' Lavretsky went on thinking, 'let me be sobered by the sameness of life here, let me be soothed and made ready, so that I may learn to do my duty without haste.' And again he fell to listening to the silence, expecting nothing—and at the same time constantly expecting something; the silence enfolded him on all sides, the sun moved calmly in the peaceful blue sky, and the clouds sailed calmly across it; they seemed to know why and whither they were sailing. At this same time in other places on the earth there is the seething, the bustle, the clash of life; life here slipped by noiseless, as water over marshy grass; and even till evening Lavretsky could not tear himself from the contemplation of this life as it passed and glided by; sorrow for the past was melting in his soul like snow in spring, and strange to say, never had the feeling of home been so deep and strong within him.

21

In the course of a fortnight, Fedor Ivanitch had brought Glafira Petrovna's little house into order and had cleared the court-yard and the garden. From Lavriky comfortable furniture was sent him; from the town, wine, books, and papers; horses made their appearance in the stable; in brief Fedor provided himself with everything necessary and began to live —not precisely after the manner of a country landowner, nor precisely after the manner of a hermit. His days passed monotonously; but he was not bored though he saw no one; he set diligently and attentively to work at farming his estate, rode about the neighbourhood and did some reading. He read little, however; he found it pleasanter to listen to the tales of old Anton. Lavretsky usually sat at the window with a pipe and a cup of cold tea. Anton stood at the door, his hands crossed behind him, and began upon his slow, deliberate stories of old times, of those fabulous times when oats and rye were not sold by measure, but in great sacks, at two or three farthings a sack; when there were impassable forests, virgin steppes stretching on every side, even close to the town. 'And now,' complained the old man, whose eightieth year had passed, 'there has been so much clearing, so much ploughing everywhere, there's nowhere you may drive now.' Anton used to tell many stories, too, of his mistress, Glafira Petrovna; how prudent and saving she was; how a certain gentleman, a young neighbour, had paid her court, and used to ride over to see her, and how she was even pleased to put on her best cap, with ribbons of salmon colour, and her yellow gown of *tru-tru lévantine* for him; but how, later on, she had been angry with the gentleman neighbour for his unseemly inquiry, 'What, madam, pray, might be your fortune?' and had bade them refuse him the house; and how it was then that she had given directions that, after her decease, everything to the last rag should pass to Fedor Ivanitch. And, indeed, Lavretsky found all his aunt's household goods intact, not excepting the best cap with ribbons of salmon colour, and the yellow gown of *tru-tru lévantine*. Of old papers and interesting documents, upon which Lavretsky had reckoned, there seemed no trace,

except one old book, in which his grandfather, Piotr Andreitch, had inscribed in one place, 'Celebration in the city of
Saint Petersburg of the peace, concluded with the Turkish
empire by his Excellency Prince Alexander Alexandrovitch
Prozorovsky'; in another place a recipe for a pectoral decoction with the comment, 'This recipe was given to the general's
lady, Prascovya Federovna Soltikov, by the chief priest of the
Church of the Life-giving Trinity, Fedor Avksentyevitch'; in
another, a piece of political news of this kind: 'Somewhat less
talk of the French tigers'; and next this entry: 'In the *Moscow
Gazette* an announcement of the death of Mr Senior-Major
Mihal Petrovitch Kolitchev. Is not this the son of Piotr
Vassilyevitch Kolitchev?' Lavretsky found also some old
calendars and dream-books, and the mysterious work of
Ambodik; many were the memories stirred by the well-
known, but long-forgotten *Symbols and Emblems*. In Glafira
Petrovna's little dressing-table, Lavretsky found a small
packet, tied up with black ribbon, sealed with black sealing
wax, and thrust away in the very farthest corner of the
drawer. In the parcel there lay face to face a portrait, in pastel,
of his father in his youth, with effeminate curls straying over
his brow, with almond-shaped languid eyes and parted lips,
and a portrait, almost effaced, of a pale woman in a white
dress with a white rose in her hand—his mother. Of herself,
Glafira Petrovna had never allowed a portrait to be taken.
'I, myself, little father, Fedor Ivanitch,' Anton used to tell
Lavretsky, 'though I did not then live in the master's house,
still I can remember your great-grandfather, Andrey Afanas-
yevitch, seeing that I had come to my eighteenth year when
he died. Once I met him in the garden, and my knees were
knocking with fright indeed; however, he did nothing, only
asked me my name, and sent me into his room for his pocket-
handkerchief. He was a gentleman—how shall I tell you—he
didn't look on any one as better than himself. For your great-
grandfather had, I do assure you, a magic amulet; a monk
from Mount Athos made him a present of this amulet. And
he told him, this monk did, "It's for your kindness, Boyar, I
give you this; wear it, and you need not fear judgment."
Well, but there, little father, we know what those times were
like; what the master fancied doing, that he did. Sometimes,

if even some gentleman saw fit to cross him in anything, he would just stare at him and say, "You swim in shallow water"; that was his favourite saying. And he lived, your great-grandfather of blessed memory, in a small log-house; and what goods he left behind him, what silver, and stores of all kinds! All the storehouses were full and overflowing. He was a manager. That very decanter, that you were pleased to admire, was his; he used to drink brandy out of it. But there was your grandfather, Piotr Andreitch, built himself a palace of stone, but he never grew rich; everything with him went badly, and he lived worse than his father by far, and he got no pleasure from it for himself, but spent all his money, and now there is nothing to remember him by—not a silver spoon has come down from him, and we have Glafira Petrovna's management to thank for all that is saved.'

'But is it true,' Lavretsky interrupted him, 'they called her the old witch?'

'What sort of people called her so, I should like to know!' replied Anton with an air of displeasure.

'And, little father,' the old man one day found courage to ask, 'what about our mistress, where is she pleased to fix her residence?'

'I am separated from my wife,' Lavretsky answered with an effort, 'please do not ask questions about her.'

'Yes, sir,' replied the old man mournfully.

After three weeks had passed by, Lavretsky rode into O—— to the Kalitins', and spent an evening with them. Lemm was there; Lavretsky took a great liking to him. Although, thanks to his father, he played no instrument, he was passionately fond of music, real classical music. Panshin was not at the Kalitins' that evening. The governor had sent him off to some place out of the town. Lisa played alone and very correctly; Lemm woke up, got excited, twisted a piece of paper into a roll, and conducted. Marya Dmitrievna laughed at first, as she looked at him, later on she went off to bed; in her own words, Beethoven was too agitating for her nerves. At midnight Lavretsky accompanied Lemm to his lodging and stopped there with him till three o'clock in the morning. Lemm talked a great deal; his bent figure grew erect, his eyes opened wide and flashed fire; his hair even stood up on his forehead. It was so long since any one had shown him any sympathy, and Lavretsky was obviously interested in him, he was plying him with sympathetic and attentive questions. This touched the old man; he ended by showing the visitor his music, played and even sang in a faded voice some extracts from his works, among others the whole of Schiller's ballad, *Fridolin*, set by him to music. Lavretsky admired it, made him repeat some passages, and at parting, invited him to stay a few days with him. Lemm, as he accompanied him as far as the street, agreed at once, and warmly pressed his hand; but, when he was left standing alone in the fresh, damp air, in the just dawning sunrise, he looked round him, shuddered, shrank into himself, and crept up to his little room, with a guilty air. '*Ich bin wohl nicht klug*' (I must be out of my senses), he muttered, as he lay down in his hard short bed. He tried to say that he was ill, a few days later, when Lavretsky drove over to fetch him in an open carriage; but Fedor Ivanitch went up into his room and managed to persuade him. What produced the most powerful effect upon Lemm was the circumstance that Lavretsky had ordered a piano from town to be sent into the country expressly for him. They set off together to the Kalitins' and spent the evening with them, but not so pleasantly as on the last occasion. Panshin was there, he talked a great deal about his expedition, and very amusingly mimicked and described the country gentry he had seen; Lavretsky laughed, but Lemm would not come out of his corner, and sat silent, slightly tremulous all over like a spider, looking dull and sullen, and he only revived when Lavretsky began to take leave. Even when he was sitting in the carriage, the old man was still shy and constrained; but the warm soft air, the light breeze, and the light shadows, the scent of the grass and the birch-buds, the peaceful light of the starlit, moonless night, the pleasant tramp and snort of the horses—all the witchery of the roadside, the spring and the night, sank into the poor German's soul, and he was himself the first to begin a conversation with Lavretsky.

✳ *22* ✳

He began talking about music, about Lisa, then of music again. He seemed to enunciate his words more slowly when he spoke of Lisa. Lavretsky turned the conversation on his compositions, and half in jest, offered to write him a libretto.

'H'm, a libretto?' replied Lemm; 'no, that is not in my line; I have not now the liveliness, the play of the imagination, which is needed for an opera; I have lost too much of my power . . . But if I were still able to do something,—I should be contented with a song; of course I should like to have beautiful words . . .'

He ceased speaking, and sat a long while motionless, his eyes lifted to the heavens.

'For instance,' he said at last, 'something in this way: "Ye stars, ye pure stars!"'

Lavretsky turned his face slightly towards him and began to look at him.

' "Ye stars, pure stars," ' repeated Lemm. . . . ' "You look down upon the righteous and the guilty alike . . . but only the pure in heart,"—or something of that kind—"comprehend you"—that is, no—"love you." But I am not a poet. I'm not equal to it! Something of that kind, though, something lofty.'

Lemm pushed his hat on to the back of his head; in the dim twilight of the clear night his face looked paler and younger.

' "And you too," ' he continued, his voice gradually sinking, ' "ye know who loves, who can love, because ye, pure ones, ye alone can comfort" . . . No, that's not it at all! I am not a poet,' he said, 'but something of that sort.'

'I am sorry I am not a poet,' observed Lavretsky.

'Vain dreams!' replied Lemm, and he buried himself in the corner of the carriage. He closed his eyes as though he were disposing himself to sleep.

A few instants passed . . . Lavretsky listened . . . ' "Stars, pure stars, love," ' muttered the old man.

'Love,' Lavretsky repeated to himself. He sank into thought—and his heart grew heavy.

'That is beautiful music you have set to *Fridolin*, Christopher Fedoritch,' he said aloud, 'but what do you suppose, did that Fridolin do, after the Count had presented him to his wife . . . became her love, eh?'

'You think so,' replied Lemm, 'probably because experience,'—he stopped suddenly and turned away in confusion. Lavretsky laughed constrainedly, and also turned away and began gazing at the road.

The stars had begun to grow paler and the sky had turned grey when the carriage drove up to the steps of the little house in Vassilyevskoe. Lavretsky conducted his guest to the room prepared for him, returned to his study and sat down before the window. In the garden a nightingale was singing its last song before dawn, Lavretsky remembered that a nightingale had sung in the garden at the Kalitins'; he remembered, too, the soft stir in Lisa's eyes, as at its first notes, they turned towards the dark window. He began to think of her, and his heart was calm again. 'Pure maiden,' he murmured half-aloud: 'pure stars,' he added with a smile, and went peacefully to bed.

But Lemm sat a long while on his bed, a music-book on his knees. He felt as though sweet, unheard melody was haunting him; already he was all aglow and astir, already he felt the languor and sweetness of its presence . . . but he could not reach it.

'Neither poet nor musician!' he muttered at last . . . And his tired head sank wearily on to the pillows.

* 23 *

The next morning the master of the house and his guest drank tea in the garden under an old lime-tree.

'Maestro!' said Lavretsky among other things, 'you will soon have to compose a triumphal cantata.'

'On what occasion?'

'For the nuptials of Mr Panshin and Lisa. Did you notice what attention he paid her yesterday? It seems as though things were in a fair way with them already.'

'That will never be!' cried Lemm.

'Why?'

'Because it is impossible. Though, indeed,' he added after a short pause, 'everything is possible in this world. Especially here among you in Russia.'

'We will leave Russia out of the question for a time; but what do you find amiss in this match?'

'Everything is amiss, everything. Lisaveta Mihalovna is a girl of high principles, serious, of lofty feelings, and he . . . he is a dilettante, in a word.'

'But suppose she loves him?'

Lemm got up from the bench.

'No, she does not love him, that is to say, she is very pure in heart, and does not know herself what it means . . . love. Madame von Kalitin tells her that he is a fine young man, and she obeys Madame von Kalitin because she is still quite a child, though she is nineteen; she says her prayers in the morning and in the evening—and that is very well; but she does not love him. She can only love what is beautiful, and he is not, that is, his soul is not beautiful.'

Lemm uttered this whole speech coherently and with fire, walking with little steps to and fro before the tea-table, and running his eyes over the ground.

'Dearest maestro!' cried Lavretsky suddenly, 'it strikes me you are in love with my cousin yourself.'

Lemm stopped short all at once.

'I beg you,' he began in an uncertain voice, 'do not make fun of me like that. I am not crazy; I look towards the dark grave, not towards a rosy future.'

Lavretsky felt sorry for the old man; he begged his pardon. After morning tea, Lemm played him his cantata, and after dinner, at Lavretsky's initiative, there was again talk of Lisa. Lavretsky listened to him with attention and curiosity.

'What do you say, Christopher Fedoritch,' he said at last, 'you see everything here seems in good order now, and the garden is in full bloom, couldn't we invite her over here for a day with her mother and my old aunt . . . eh? Would you like it?'

Lemm bent his head over his plate.

'Invite her,' he murmured, scarcely audibly.

'But Panshin isn't wanted?'

'No, he isn't wanted,' rejoined the old man with an almost child-like smile.

Two days later Fedor Ivanitch set off to the town to see the Kalitins.

* *24* *

He found them all at home, but he did not at once disclose his plan to them; he wanted to discuss it first with Lisa alone. Fortune favoured him; they were left alone in the drawing-room. They had some talk; she had had time by now to grow used to him—and she was not shy as a rule with any one. He listened to her, watched her, and mentally repeated Lemm's words, and agreed with them. It sometimes happens that two people who are acquainted, but not on intimate terms with one another, all of a sudden grow rapidly more intimate in a few minutes, and the consciousness of this greater intimacy is at once expressed in their eyes, in their soft and affectionate smiles, and in their very gestures. This was exactly what came to pass with Lavretsky and Lisa. 'So he is like that,' was her thought, as she turned a friendly glance on him; 'so you are like that,' he too was thinking. And so he was not very much surprised when she informed him, not without a little falter-ing, however, that she had long wished to say something to him, but she was afraid of offending him.

'Don't be afraid; tell me,' he replied, and stood still before her.

Lisa raised her clear eyes to him.

'You are so good,' she began, and at the same time, she thought: 'Yes, I am sure he is good' . . . 'you will forgive me, I ought not to dare to speak of it to you . . . but—how could you . . . why did you separate from your wife?'

Lavretsky shuddered: he looked at Lisa, and sat down near her.

'My child,' he began, 'I beg you, do not touch upon that wound; your hands are tender, but it will hurt me all the same.'

'I know,' Lisa went on, as though she did not hear him,

'she has been to blame towards you. I don't want to defend her; but what God has joined, how can you put asunder?'

'Our convictions on that subject are too different, Lisaveta Mihalovna,' Lavretsky observed, rather sharply; 'we cannot understand one another.'

Lisa grew paler: her whole frame was trembling slightly; but she was not silenced.

'You must forgive,' she murmured softly, 'if you wish to be forgiven.'

'Forgive!' broke in Lavretsky. 'Ought you not first to know whom you are interceding for? Forgive that woman, take her back into my home, that empty, heartless creature! And who told you she wants to return to me? She is perfectly contented with her position, I can assure you. . . . But what a subject to discuss here! Her name ought never to be uttered by you. You are too pure, you are not capable of understanding such a creature.'

'Why abuse her?' Lisa articulated with an effort. The trembling of her hands was perceptible now. 'You left her yourself, Fedor Ivanitch.'

'But I tell you,' retorted Lavretsky with an involuntary outburst of impatience, 'you don't know what that woman is!'

'Then why did you marry her?' whispered Lisa, and her eyes fell.

Lavretsky got up quickly from his seat.

'Why did I marry her? I was young and inexperienced; I was deceived, I was carried away by a beautiful exterior. I knew no women. I knew nothing. God grant you may make a happier marriage! But let me tell you, you can be sure of nothing.'

'I too might be unhappy,' said Lisa (her voice had begun to be unsteady), 'but then I ought to submit, I don't know how to say it; but if we do not submit'——

Lavretsky clenched his hands and stamped with his foot.

'Don't be angry, forgive me,' Lisa faltered hurriedly.

At that instant Marya Dmitrievna came in. Lisa got up and was going away.

'Stop a minute,' Lavretsky cried after her unexpectedly. 'I have a great favour to beg of your mother and you; to pay me a visit in my new abode. You know, I have had a piano

[73]

sent over; Lemm is staying with me; the lilac is in flower now; you will get a breath of country air, and you can return the same day—will you consent?' Lisa looked towards her mother; Marya Dmitrievna was assuming an expression of suffering; but Lavretsky did not give her time to open her mouth; he at once kissed both her hands. Marya Dmitrievna, who was always susceptible to demonstrations of feeling, and did not at all anticipate such effusiveness from the 'dolt', was melted and gave her consent. While she was deliberating which day to fix, Lavretsky went up to Lisa, and, still greatly moved, whispered to her aside: 'Thank you, you are a good girl; I was to blame.' And her pale face glowed with a bright, shy smile; her eyes smiled too—up to that instant she had been afraid she had offended him.

'Vladimir Nikolaitch can come with us?' inquired Marya Dmitrievna.

'Yes,' replied Lavretsky, 'but would it not be better to be just a family party?'

'Well, you know, it seems,' began Marya Dmitrievna.

'But as you please,' she added.

It was decided to take Lenotchka and Shurotchka. Marfa Timofyevna refused to join in the expedition.

'It is hard for me, my darling,' she said, 'to give my old bones a shaking; and to be sure there's nowhere for me to sleep at your place: besides, I can't sleep in a strange bed. Let the young folks go frolicking.'

Lavretsky did not succeed in being alone again with Lisa; but he looked at her in such a way that she felt her heart at rest, and a little ashamed, and sorry for him. He pressed her hand warmly at parting; left alone, she fell to musing.

* 25 *

When Lavretsky reached home, he was met at the door of the drawing-room by a tall, thin man, in a thread-bare blue coat, with a wrinkled, but lively face, with dishevelled grey whiskers, a long straight nose, and small fiery eyes. This was

Mihalevitch, who had been his friend at the university. Lavretsky did not at first recognise him, but embraced him warmly directly he told his name. They had not met since their Moscow days. Torrents of exclamations and questions followed; long-buried recollections were brought to light. Hurriedly smoking pipe after pipe, tossing off tea at a gulp, and gesticulating with his long hands, Mihalevitch related his adventures to Lavretsky; there was nothing very inspiriting in them, he could not boast of success in his undertakings—but he was constantly laughing a hoarse, nervous laugh. A month previously he had received a position in the private counting-house of a spirit-tax contractor, two hundred and fifty miles from the town of O——, and hearing of Lavretsky's return from abroad he had turned out of his way so as to see his old friend. Mihalevitch talked as impetuously as in his youth; made as much noise and was as effervescent as of old. Lavretsky was about to acquaint him with his position, but Mihalevitch interrupted him, muttering hurriedly, 'I have heard, my dear fellow, I have heard—who could have anticipated it?' and at once turned the conversation upon general subjects.

'I must set off to-morrow, my dear fellow,' he observed; 'to-day if you will exuse it, we will sit up late. I want above all to know what you are like, what are your views and convictions, what you have become, what life has taught you.' (Mihalevitch still preserved the phraseology of 1830.) 'As for me, I have changed in much; the waves of life have broken over my breast—who was it said that?—though in what is important, essential I have not changed; I believe as of old in the good, the true: but I do not only believe—I have faith now, yes, I have faith, faith. Listen, you know I write verses; there is no poetry in them, but there is truth. I will read you aloud my last poem; I have expressed my truest convictions in it. Listen.' Mihalevitch fell to reading his poem: it was rather long, and ended with the following lines:

> I gave myself to new feelings with all my heart,
> And my soul became as a child's!
> And I have burnt all I adored,
> And now adore all that I burnt.

As he uttered the two last lines, Mihalevitch all but shed tears; a slight spasm—the sign of deep emotion—passed over his wide mouth, his ugly face lighted up. Lavretsky listened, and listened to him—and the spirit of antagonism was aroused in him; he was irritated by the ever-ready enthusiasm of the Moscow student, perpetually at boiling-point. Before a quarter of an hour had elapsed a heated argument had broken out between them, one of these endless arguments, of which only Russians are capable. After a separation of many years spent in two different worlds, with no clear understanding of the other's ideas or even of their own, catching at words and replying only in words, they disputed about the most abstract subjects, and they disputed as though it were a matter of life and death for both: they shouted and vociferated so that every-one in the house was startled, and poor Lemm, who had locked himself up in his room directly after Mihalevitch arrived, was bewildered, and began even to feel vaguely alarmed.

'What are you after all? a pessimist?' cried Mihalevitch at one o'clock in the night.

'Are pessimists usually like this?' replied Lavretsky. 'They are usually all pale and sickly—would you like me to lift you with one hand?'

'Well, if you are not a pessimist you are a *scepteec*, that's still worse.' Mihalevitch's talk had a strong flavour of his mother-country, Little Russia. 'And what right have you to be a *scepteec*? You have had ill-luck in life, let us admit; that was not your fault; you were born with a passionate loving heart, and you were unnaturally kept out of the society of women: the first woman you came across was bound to deceive you.'

'She deceived you too,' observed Lavretsky grimly.

'Granted, granted; I was the tool of destiny in it—what nonsense I talk, though—there is no such thing as destiny; it is an old habit of expressing things inexactly. But what does that prove?'

'It proves this, that they distorted me from my child-hood.'

'Well, it's for you to straighten yourself! What's the good of being a man, a male animal? And however that may be, is it possible, is it permissible, to reduce a personal, so to speak, fact to a general law, to an infallible principle?'

'How a principle?' interrupted Lavretsky; 'I don't admit—'

'No, it is your principle, your principle,' Mihalevitch interrupted in his turn.

'You are an egoist, that's what it is!' he was thundering an hour later: 'you wanted personal happiness, you wanted enjoyment in life, you wanted to live only for yourself.'

'What do you mean by personal happiness?'

'And everything deceived you; everything crumbled away under your feet.'

'What do you mean by personal happiness, I ask you?'

'And it was bound to crumble away. Either you sought support where it could not be found, or you built your house on shifting sands, or—'

'Speak more plainly, *or* I can't understand you.'

'Or—you may laugh if you like—or you had no faith, no warmth of heart; intellect, nothing but one farthing's worth of intellect . . . you are simply a pitiful, antiquated Voltairean, that's what you are!'

'I'm a Voltairean?'

'Yes, like your father, and you yourself do not suspect it.'

'After that,' exclaimed Lavretsky, 'I have the right to call you a fanatic.'

'Alas!' replied Mihalevitch with a contrite air, 'I have not so far deserved such an exalted title, unhappily.'

'I have found out now what to call you,' cried the same Mihalevitch, at three o'clock in the morning. 'You are not a sceptic, nor a pessimist, nor a Voltairean, you are a loafer, and you are a vicious loafer, a conscious loafer, not a simple loafer. Simple loafers lie on the stove and do nothing because they don't know how to do anything; they don't think about anything either, but you are a man of ideas—and yet you lie on the stove; you could do something—and you do nothing; you lie idle with a full stomach and look down from above and say, "It's best to lie idle like this, because whatever people do, is all rubbish, leading to nothing." '

'And from what do you infer that I lie idle?' Lavretsky protested stoutly. 'Why do you attribute such ideas to me?'

'And, besides that, you are all, all the tribe of you,' continued Mihalevitch, 'cultivated loafers. You know which leg the German limps on, you know what's amiss with the English and the French, and your pitiful culture goes to make it worse, your shameful idleness, your abominable inactivity is justified by it. Some are even proud of it: "I'm such a clever fellow," they say, "I do nothing, while these fools are in a fuss." Yes! and there are fine gentlemen among us—though I don't say this as to you—who reduce their whole life to a kind of stupor of boredom, get used to it, live in it, like—like a mushroom in white sauce,' Mihalevitch added hastily, and he laughed at his own comparison. 'Oh! this stupor of boredom is the ruin of Russians. Ours is the age for work, and the sickening loafer' . . .

'But what is all this abuse about?' Lavretsky clamoured in his turn. 'Work—doing—you'd better say what is to be done, instead of abusing me, Desmosthenes of Poltava!'

'There, what a thing to ask! I can't tell you that, brother; that, everyone ought to know for himself,' retorted the Desmosthenes ironically. A landowner, a nobleman, and not know what to do? You have no faith, or else you would know; no faith—and no intuition.'

'Let me at least have time to breathe; you don't let me have time to look round,' Lavretsky besought him.

'Not a minute, not a second!' retorted Mihalevitch with an imperious wave of the hand. 'Not one second: death does not delay, and life ought not to delay.'

'And what a time, what a place for men to think of loafing!' he cried at four o'clock, in a voice, however, which showed signs of sleepiness; 'among us! now! in Russia! where every separate individuality has a duty resting upon him, a solemn responsibility to God, to the people, to himself. We are sleeping, and the time is slipping away; we are sleeping.' . . .

'Permit me to observe,' remarked Lavretsky, 'that we are not sleeping at present, but rather preventing others from sleeping. We are straining our throats like the cocks—listen! there is one crowing for the third time.'

This sally made Mihalevitch laugh, and calmed him down. 'Good-bye till to-morrow,' he said with a smile, and thrust his pipe into his pouch.

'Till to-morrow,' repeated Lavretsky. But the friends

talked for more than an hour longer. Their voices were no longer raised, however, and their talk was quiet, sad, friendly talk.

Mihalevitch set off the next day, in spite of all Lavretsky's efforts to keep him. Fedor Ivanitch did not succeed in persuading him to remain; but he talked to him to his heart's content. Mihalevitch, it appeared, had not a penny to bless himself with. Lavretsky had noticed with pain the evening before all the tokens and habits of years of poverty: his boots were shabby, a button was off on the back of his coat, his hands were unused to gloves, his hair wanted brushing; on his arrival, he had not even thought of asking to wash, and at supper he ate like a shark, tearing his meat in his fingers, and crunching the bones with his strong black teeth. It appeared, too, that he had made nothing out of his employment, that he now rested all his hopes on the contractor who was taking him solely in order to have an 'educated man' in his office. For all that Mihalevitch was not discouraged, but as idealist or cynic, lived on a crust of bread, sincerely rejoicing or grieving over the destinies of humanity, and his own vocation, and troubling himself very little as to how to escape dying of hunger. Mihalevitch was not married: but had been in love times beyond number, and had written poems to all the objects of his adoration; he sang with especial fervour the praises of a mysterious black-tressed 'noble Polish lady'. There were rumours, it is true, that this 'noble Polish lady' was a simple Jewess, very well known to a good many cavalry officers—but, after all, what do you think—does it really make any difference?

With Lemm, Mihalevitch did not get on; his noisy talk and brusque manners scared the German, who was unused to such behaviour. One poor devil detects another by instinct at once, but in old age he rarely gets on with him, and that is hardly astonishing, he has nothing to share with him, not even hopes.

Before setting off, Mihalevitch had another long discussion with Lavretsky, foretold his ruin, if he did not see the error of his ways, exhorted him to devote himself seriously to the welfare of his peasants, and pointed to himself as an example, saying that he had been purified in the furnace of suffering; and in the same breath called himself several times a happy man, comparing himself with the fowl of the air and the lily of the field.

'A black lily, any way,' observed Lavretsky.

'Ah, brother, don't be a snob!' retorted Mihalevitch, good-naturedly, 'but thank God rather that there is pure plebeian blood in your veins too. But I see you want some pure, heavenly creature to draw you out of your apathy.'

'Thanks, brother,' remarked Lavretsky. 'I have had quite enough of those heavenly creatures.'

'Silence, ceeneec!' cried Mihalevitch.

'Cynic,' Lavretsky corrected him.

'Ceeneec, just so,' repeated Mihalevitch unabashed.

Even when he had taken his seat in the carriage, to which his flat, yellow, strangely light trunk was carried, he still talked; muffled in a kind of Spanish cloak with a collar, brown with age, and a clasp of two lion's paws; he went on developing his views on the destiny of Russia, and waving his swarthy hand in the air, as though he were sowing the seeds of her future prosperity. The horses started at last.

'Remember my three last words,' he cried, thrusting his whole body out of the carriage and balancing so, 'Religion, progress, humanity! . . . Farewell.'

His head, with a foraging cap pulled down over his eyes, disappeared. Lavretsky was left standing alone on the steps, and he gazed steadily into the distance along the road till the carriage disappeared out of sight. 'Perhaps he is right, after all,' he thought as he went back into the house; 'perhaps I am a loafer.' Many of Mihalevitch's words had sunk irresistibly into his heart, though he had disputed and disagreed with him. If a man only has a good heart, no one can resist him.

✳ *26* ✳

Two days later, Marya Dmitrievna visted Vassilyevskoe according to her promise, with all her young people. The little girls ran at once into the garden, while Marya Dmitrievna languidly walked through the rooms and languidly admired everything. She regarded her visit to Lavretsky as a sign of great condescension, almost as a deed of charity. She smiled graciously when Anton and Apraxya kissed her hand in the old-fashioned house-servants' style; and in a weak voice, speaking through her nose, asked for some tea. To the great vexation of Anton, who had put on knitted white gloves for the purpose, tea was not handed to the grand lady visitor by him, but by Lavretsky's hired valet, who in the old man's words, had not a notion of what was proper. To make up for this, Anton resumed his rights at dinner: he took up a firm position behind Marya Dmitrievna's chair, and would not surrender his post to any one. The appearance of guests after so long an interval at Vassilyevskoe fluttered and delighted the old man; it was a pleasure to him to see that his master was acquainted with such fine gentlefolk. He was not, however, the only one who was fluttered that day; Lemm, too, was in agitation. He had put on a rather short snuff-coloured coat with a swallow-tail, and tied his neckhandkerchief stiffly, and he kept incessantly coughing and making way for people with a cordial and affable air. Lavretsky noticed with pleasure that his relations with Lisa were becoming more intimate; she had held out her hand to him affectionately directly she came in. After dinner Lemm drew out of his coat-tail pocket, into which he had continually been fumbling, a small roll of music-paper and compressing his lips he laid it without speaking on the pianoforte. It was a song composed by him the evening before, to some old-fashioned German words, in which mention was made of the stars. Lisa sat down at once to the piano and played at sight the song. . . . Alas! the music turned out to be complicated and painfully strained; it was clear that the composer had striven to express something passionate and deep, but nothing had come of it; the effort had remained an effort. Lavretsky and Lisa both felt this, and Lemm understood it. Without uttering a single word, he put his song back into his pocket, and in reply to Lisa's proposal to play it again, he only shook his head and said significantly: 'Now—enough!' and shrinking into himself he turned away.

Towards evening the whole party went out to fish. In the pond behind the garden there were plenty of carp and ground-lings. Marya Dmitrievna was put in an arm-chair near the bank, in the shade, with a rug under her feet and the best line was given to her. Anton as an old experienced angler offered her his services. He zealously put on the worms, and clapped his hand on them, spat on them and even threw in the line with a graceful forward swing of his whole body. Marya Dmitrievna spoke of him the same day to Fedor Ivanitch in the following phrase, in boarding-school French: '*Il n'y a plus maintenant de ces gens comme ça, comme autrefois.*' Lemm with the two little girls went off further to the dam of the pond; Lavretsky took up his position near Lisa. The fish were continually biting, the carp were constantly flashing in the air with golden and silvery sides as they were drawn in; the cries of pleasure of the little girls were incessant, even Marya Dmitrievna uttered a little feminine shriek on two occasions. The fewest fish were caught by Lavretsky and Lisa; probably this was because they paid less attention than the others to the angling, and allowed their floats to swim back right up to the bank. The high reddish reeds rustled quietly around, the still water shone quietly before them, and quietly too they talked together. Lisa was standing on a small raft; Lavretsky sat on the inclined trunk of a willow; Lisa wore a white gown, tied round the waist with a broad ribbon, also white; her straw hat was hanging on one hand, and in the other with some effort she held up the crooked rod. Lavretsky gazed at her pure, somewhat severe profile, at her hair drawn back behind her ears, at her soft cheeks, which glowed like a little child's, and thought, 'Oh, how sweet you are, bending over my pond!' Lisa did not turn to him, but looked at the water, half frowning, to keep the sun out of her eyes, half smiling. The shade of the lime-tree near fell upon both.

'Do you know,' began Lavretsky, 'I have been thinking over our last conversation a great deal, and have come to the conclusion that you are exceedingly good.'

'That was not at all my intention in—' Lisa was beginning to reply, and she was overcome with embarrassment.

'You are good,' repeated Lavretsky. 'I am a rough fellow, but I feel that everyone must love you. There's Lemm for instance; he is simply in love with you.'

Lisa's brows did not exactly frown, they contracted slightly; it always happened with her when she heard something disagreeable to her.

'I was very sorry for him to-day,' Lavretsky added, 'with his unsuccessful song. To be young and to fail is bearable; but to be old and not be successful is hard to bear. And how mortifying it is to feel that one's forces are deserting one! It is hard for an old man to bear such blows! . . . Be careful, you have a bite. . . . They say,' added Lavretsky after a short pause, 'that Vladimir Nikolaitch has written a very pretty song.'

'Yes,' replied Lisa, 'it is only a trifle, but not bad.'

'And what do you think,' inquired Lavretsky; 'is he a good musician?'

'I think he has great talent for music; but so far he has not worked at it, as he should.'

'Ah! And is he a good sort of man?'

Lisa laughed and glanced quickly at Fedor Ivanitch.

'What a queer question!' she exclaimed, drawing up her line and throwing it in again further off.

'Why is it queer? I ask you about him, as one who has only lately come here, as a relation.'

'A relation?'

'Yes. I am, it seems, a sort of uncle of yours?'

'Vladimir Nikolaitch has a good heart,' said Lisa, 'and he is clever; *maman* likes him very much'.

'And do you like him?'

'He is nice; why should I not like him?'

'Ah!' Lavretsky uttered and ceased speaking. A half-mournful, half-ironical expression passed over his face. His steadfast gaze embarrassed Lisa, but she went on smiling.—

'Well God grant them happiness!' he muttered at last, as though to himself, and turned away his head.

Lisa flushed.

'You are mistaken, Fedor Ivanitch,' she said: 'you are wrong in thinking. . . . But don't you like Vladimir Niko-laitch?' she asked suddenly.

'No, I don't.'

'Why?'

'I think he has no heart.'

The smile left Lisa's face.

'It is your habit to judge people severely,' she observed after a long silence.

'I don't think it is. What right have I to judge others

severely, do you suppose, when I must ask for indulgence myself? Or have you forgotten that I am a laughing stock to everyone, who is not too indifferent even to scoff? . . . By the way,' he added, 'did you keep your promise?'

'What promise?'

'Did you pray for me?'

'Yes, I prayed for you, and I pray for you every day. But please do not speak lightly of that.'

Lavretsky began to assure Lisa that the idea of doing so had never entered his head, that he had the deepest reverence for every conviction; then he went off into a discourse upon religion, its significance in the history of mankind, the significance of Christianity.

'One must be a Christian,' observed Lisa, not without some effort, 'not so as to know the divine . . . and the . . . earthly, but because every man has to die.'

Lavretsky raised his eyes in involuntary astonishment upon Lisa and met her gaze.

'What a strange saying you have just uttered!' he said.

'It is not my saying,' she replied.

'Not yours. . . . But what made you speak of death?'

'I don't know. I often think of it.'

'Often?'

'Yes.'

'One would not suppose so, looking at you now; you have such a bright, happy face, you are smiling.'

'Yes, I am very happy just now,' replied Lisa simply.

Lavretsky would have liked to seize both her hands, and press them warmly.

'Lisa, Lisa!' cried Marya Dmitrievna, 'do come here, and look what a fine carp I have caught.'

'In a minute, *maman*,' replied Lisa, and went towards her, but Lavretsky remained sitting on his willow. 'I talk to her just as if life were not over for me,' he thought. As she went away, Lisa hung her hat on a twig; with strange, almost tender emotion, Lavretsky looked at the hat, and its long rather crumpled ribbons. Lisa soon came back to him, and again took her stand on the platform.

'What makes you think Vladimir Nikolaitch has no heart?' she asked a few minutes later.

'I have told you already that I may be mistaken; time will show, however.'

Lisa grew thoughtful. Lavretsky began to tell her about his life at Vassilyevskoe, about Mihalevitch, and about Anton; he felt a need to talk to Lisa, to share with her everything that was passing in his heart; she listened so sweetly, so attentively; her few replies and observations seemed to him so simple and so intelligent. He even told her so.

Lisa was surprised.

'Really?' she said; 'I thought that I was like my maid, Nastya, I had no words of my own. She said one day to her sweetheart, "You must be dull with me; you always talk so finely to me, and I have no words of my own."'

'And thank God for it!' thought Lavretsky.

* 27 *

Meanwhile the evening had come on, Marya Dmitrievna expressed a desire to return home, and the little girls were with difficulty torn away from the pond, and made ready. Lavretsky declared that he would escort his guests half-way, and ordered his horse to be saddled. As he was handing Marya Dmitrievna into the coach, he bethought himself of Lemm; but the old man could nowhere be found. He had disappeared directly after the angling was over. Anton, with an energy remarkable for his years, slammed the doors, and called sharply, 'Go on, coachman!' The coach started. Marya Dmitrievna and Lisa were seated in the back seat; the children and their maid in the front. The evening was warm and still, and the windows were open on both sides. Lavretsky trotted near the coach on the side of Lisa, with his arm leaning on the door—he had thrown the reins on the neck of his smoothly-pacing horse—and now and then he exchanged a few words with the young girl. The glow of sunset was disappearing; night came on, but the air seemed to grow even warmer. Marya Dmitrievna was soon slumbering, the little girls and the maid fell asleep also. The coach rolled swiftly and smoothly along; Lisa was bending forward, she felt happy; the rising moon lighted up her face, the fragrant night breeze breathed on her eyes and cheeks. Her hand rested on the coach door near Lavretsky's hand. And he was happy; borne along in the still warmth of the night, never taking his eyes off the good young face, listening to the young voice that was melodious even in a whisper, as it spoke of simple, good things, he did not even notice that he had gone more than half-way. He did not want to wake Marya Dmitrievna, he lightly pressed Lisa's hand and said, 'I think we are friends now, aren't we?' She nodded, he stopped his horse, and the coach rolled away, lightly swaying and oscillating up and down; Lavretsky turned homeward at a walking pace. The witchery of the summer night enfolded him; all around him seemed suddenly so strange—and at the same time so long known, so sweetly familiar. Everywhere near and afar—and one could see into the far distance, though the eye could not make out clearly much of what was seen—all was at peace; youthful, blossoming life seemed expressed in this deep peace. Lavretsky's horse stepped out bravely, swaying evenly to right and left; its great black shadow moved along beside it. There was something strangely sweet in the tramp of its hoofs, a strange charm in the ringing cry of the quails. The stars were lost in a bright mist; the moon, not yet at the full, shone with steady brilliance; its light was shed in an azure stream over the sky, and fell in patches of smoky gold on the thin clouds as they drifted near. The freshness of the air drew a slight moisture into the eyes, sweetly folded all the limbs, and flowed freely into the lungs. Lavretsky rejoiced in it, and was glad at his own rejoicing. 'Come, we are still alive,' he thought; 'we have not been altogether destroyed by'—he did not say—by whom or by what. Then he fell to thinking of Lisa, that she could hardly love Panshin, that if he had met her under different circumstances—God knows what might have come of it; that he understood Lemm, though Lisa had no words of 'her own'; but that, he thought, was not true; she had words of her own. 'Don't speak lightly of that,' came back to Lavretsky's mind. He rode a long way with his head bent in thought, then drawing himself up, he slowly repeated aloud:

'And I have burnt all I adored,
And now adore all that I burnt.'

Then he gave his horse a switch with the whip, and galloped all the way home.

Dismounting from his horse, he looked round for the last time with an involuntary smile of gratitude. Night, still, kindly night stretched over hills and valleys; from afar, out of its fragrant depths—God knows whence—whether from the heavens or the earth—rose a soft, gentle warmth. Lavretsky sent a last greeting to Lisa, and ran up the steps.

The next day passed rather dully. Rain was falling from early morning; Lemm wore a scowl, and kept more and more tightly compressing his lips, as though he had taken an oath never to open them again. When he went to his room, Lavretsky took up to bed with him a whole bundle of French newspapers, which had been lying for more than a fortnight on his table unopened. He began indifferently to tear open the wrappings, and glanced hastily over the columns of the newspapers—in which, however, there was nothing new. He was just about to throw them down—and all at once he leaped out of bed as if he had been stung. In an article in one of the papers, M. Jules, with whom we are already familiar, communicated to his readers a 'mournful intelligence, that charming, fascinating Moscow lady', he wrote, 'one of the queens of fashion, who adorned Parisian salons, Madame de Lavretsky, had died almost suddenly, and this intelligence, unhappily only too well-founded, had only just reached him, M. Jules. He was,' so he continued, 'he might say a friend of the deceased.'

Lavretsky dressed, went out into the garden, and till morning he walked up and down the same path.

* *28* *

The next morning, over the tea, Lemm asked Lavretsky to let him have the horses to return to town. 'It's time for me to set to work, that is, to my lessons,' observed the old man.

'Besides, I am only wasting time here.' Lavretsky did not reply at once; he seemed abstracted. 'Very good,' he said at last; 'I will come with you myself.' Unaided by the servants, Lemm, groaning and wrathful, packed his small box and tore up and burnt a few sheets of music-paper. The horses were harnessed. As he came out of his own room, Lavretsky put the paper he had read last night in his pocket. During the whole course of the journey both Lemm and Lavretsky spoke little to one another; each was occupied with his own thoughts, and each was glad not to be disturbed by the other; and they parted rather coolly, which is often the way, however, with friends in Russia. Lavretsky conducted the old man to his little house; the latter got out, took his trunk, and without holding out his hand to his friend (he was holding his trunk in both arms before his breast), without even looking at him, he said to him in Russian, 'good-bye!' 'Good-bye,' repeated Lavretsky, and bade the coachman drive to his lodging. He had taken rooms in the town of O—— . . . After writing a few letters and hastily dining, Lavretsky went to the Kalitins'. In their drawing-room he found only Panshin, who informed him that Marya Dmitrievna would be in directly, and at once, with charming cordiality, entered into conversation with him. Until that day, Panshin had always treated Lavretsky, not exactly haughtily, but at least condescendingly; but Lisa, in describing her expedition of the previous day to Panshin, had spoken of Lavretsky as an excellent and clever man, that was enough; he felt bound to make a conquest of an 'excellent man'. Panshin began with compliments to Lavretsky, with a description of the rapture in which, according to him, the whole family of Marya Dmitrievna spoke of Vassilyevskoe; and then, according to his custom, passing neatly to himself, began to talk about his pursuits, and his views on life, the world and government service; uttered a sentence or two upon the future of Russia, and the duty of rulers to keep a strict hand over the country; and at this point laughed light-heartedly at his own expense, and added that among other things he had been entrusted in Petersburg with the duty *de populariser l'idée du cadastre*. He spoke somewhat at length, passing over all difficulties with careless self-confidence, and playing with the weightiest administrative and political

questions, as a juggler plays with balls. The expressions:
'That's what I would do if I were in the government'; 'you as
a man of intelligence, will agree with me at once', were constantly on his lips. Lavretsky listened coldly to Panshin's
chatter; he did not like this handsome, clever, easily-elegant
young man, with his bright smile, affable voice, and inquisitive eyes. Panshin, with the quick insight into the feelings
of others, which was peculiar to him, soon guessed that he
was not giving his companion any special satisfaction, and
made a plausible excuse to go away, inwardly deciding that
Lavretsky might be an 'excellent man', but he was unattractive, *aigri*, and, *en somme*, rather absurd. Marya Dmitrievna
made her appearance escorted by Gedeonovsky; then Marfa
Timofyevna and Lisa came in; and after them the other mem-
bers of the household; and then the musical amateur, Madame
Byelenitsin, arrived, a little thinnish lady, with a languid,
pretty, almost childish little face, wearing a rustling dress, a
striped fan, and heavy gold bracelets. Her husband was with
her, a fat red-faced man, with large hands and feet, white eyelashes, and an immovable smile on his thick lips; his wife
never spoke to him in company, but at home in moments of
tenderness, she used to call him her little sucking-pig. Panshin
returned; the rooms were very full of people and noise. Such
a crowd was not to Lavretsky's taste; and he was particularly
irritated by Madame Byelenitsin, who kept staring at him
through her eye-glasses. He would have gone away at once
but for Lisa; he wanted to say a few words to her alone, but
for a long time he could not get a favourable opportunity, and
had to content himself with following her in secret delight
with his eyes; never had her face seemed sweeter and more
noble to him. She gained much from being near Madame
Byelenitsin. The latter was for ever fidgeting in her chair,
shrugging her narrow little shoulders, giving little girlish
giggles, and screwing up her eyes and then opening them
wide; Lisa sat quietly, looked directly at everyone and did not
laugh at all. Madame Kalitin sat down to a game of cards
with Marfa Timofyevna, Madame Byelenitsin, and Gedeonovsky, who played very slowly, and constantly made mistakes, frowning and wiping his face with his handkerchief.
Panshin assumed a melancholy air, and expressed himself in

[89]

brief, pregnant, and gloomy phrases, played the part, in fact, of the unappreciated genius, but in spite of the entreaties of Madame Byelenitsin, who was very coquettish with him, he would not consent to sing his song; he felt Lavretsky's presence a constraint. Fedor Ivanitch also spoke little; the peculiar expression of his face struck Lisa directly he came into the room; she felt at once that he had something to tell her, and though she could not herself have said why, she was afraid to question him. At last, as she was going into the next room to pour out tea, she involuntarily turned her head in his direction. He at once went after her.

'What is the matter?' she said, setting the teapot on the samovar.

'Why, have you noticed anything?' he asked.

'You are not the same to-day as I have always seen you before.'

Lavretsky bent over the table.

'I wanted,' he began, 'to tell you a piece of news, but now it is impossible. However, you can read what is marked with pencil in that article,' he added, handing her the paper he had brought with him. 'Let me ask you to keep it a secret; I will come to-morrow morning.'

Lisa was greatly bewildered. Panshin appeared in the doorway. She put the newspaper in her pocket.

'Have you read Obermann, Lisaveta Mihalovna?' Panshin asked her pensively.

Lisa made him a reply in passing, and went out of the room and upstairs. Lavretsky went back to the drawing-room and drew near the card-table. Marfa Timofyevna, flinging back the ribbons of her cap and flushing with annoyance, began to complain of her partner, Gedeonovsky, who in her words, could not play a bit.

'Card-playing, you see,' she said, 'is not so easy as talking scandal.'

The latter continued to blink and wipe his face. Lisa came into the drawing-room and sat down in a corner; Lavretsky looked at her, she looked at him, and both felt the position insufferable. He read perplexity and a kind of secret reproachfulness in her face. He could not talk to her as he would have liked to do; to remain in the same room with her, a guest among other guests, was too painful; he decided to go away. As he took leave of her, he managed to repeat that he would come to-morrow, and added that he trusted in her friendship.

'Come,' she answered with the same perplexity on her face.

Panshin brightened up at Lavretsky's departure; he began to give advice to Gedeonovsky, paid ironical attentions to Madame Bylenitsin, and at last sang his song. But with Lisa he still spoke and looked as before, impressively and rather mournfully.

Again Lavretsky did not sleep all night. He was not sad, he was not agitated, he was quite calm; but he could not sleep. He did not even remember the past; he simply looked at his life; his heart beat slowly and evenly; the hours glided by; he did not even think of sleep. Only at times the thought flashed through his brain: 'But it is not true, it is all nonsense,' and he stood still, bowed his head and again began to ponder on the life before him.

✳ *29* ✳

Marya Dmitrievna did not give Lavretsky an over-cordial welcome when he made his appearance the following day. 'Upon my word, he's always in and out,' she thought. She did not much care for him, and Panshin, under whose influence she was, had been very artful and disparaging in his praises of him the evening before. And as she did not regard him as a visitor, and did not consider it necessary to entertain a relation, almost one of the family, it came to pass that in less than half-an-hour's time he found himself walking in an avenue in the grounds with Lisa. Lenotchka and Shurotchka were running about a few paces from them in the flower-garden.

Lisa was as calm as usual but more than usually pale. She took out of her pocket and held out to Lavretsky the sheet of the newspaper folded up small.

'That is terrible!' she said.

Lavretsky made no reply.

'But perhaps it is not true, though,' added Lisa.

'That is why I asked you not to speak of it to any one.'
Lisa walked on a little.

'Tell me,' she began: 'you are not grieved? not at all?'

'I do not know myself what I feel,' replied Lavretsky.

'But you loved her once?'

'Yes.'

'Very much?'

'Yes.'

'So you are not grieved at her death?'

'She was dead to me long ago.'

'It is sinful to say that. Do not be angry with me. You call me your friend: a friend may say everything. To me it is really terrible. . . . Yesterday there was an evil look in your face. . . . Do you remember not long ago, how you abused her, and she, perhaps, at that very time was dead? It is terrible. It has been sent to you as a punishment.'

Lavretsky smiled bitterly.

'Do you think so? At least, I am now free.'

Lisa gave a slight shudder.

'Stop, do not talk like that. Of what use is your freedom to you? You ought not to be thinking of that now, but of forgiveness.'

'I forgave her long ago,' Lavretsky interposed with a gesture of the hand.

'No, that is not it,' replied Lisa, flushing. 'You did not understand me. You ought to be seeking to be forgiven.'

'To be forgiven by whom?'

'By whom? God. Who can forgive us, but God?'

Lavretsky seized her hand.

'Ah, Lisaveta Mihalovna, believe me,' he cried, 'I have been punished enough as it is. I have expiated everything already, believe me.'

'That you cannot know,' Lisa murmured in an undertone. 'You have forgotten—not long ago, when you were talking to me—you were not ready to forgive her.'

She walked in silence along the avenue.

'And what about your daughter?' Lisa asked, suddenly stopping short.

Lavretsky started.

[92]

'Oh, don't be uneasy! I have already sent letters in all directions. The future of my daughter, as you call—as you say —is assured. Do not be uneasy.'

Lisa smiled mournfully.

'But you are right,' continued Lavretsky, 'what can I do with my freedom? What good is it to me?'

'When did you get that paper?' said Lisa, without replying to his question.

'The day after your visit.'

'And is it possible you did not even shed tears?'

'No. I was thunderstruck; but where were tears to come from? Should I weep over the past? but it is utterly extinct for me! Her very fault did not destroy my happiness, but only showed me that it had never been at all. What is there to weep over now? Though indeed, who knows? I might, perhaps, have been more grieved if I had got this news a fortnight sooner.'

'A fortnight?' repeated Lisa. 'But what has happened then in the last fortnight?'

Lavretsky made no answer, and suddenly Lisa flushed even more than before.

'Yes, yes, you guess why,' Lavretsky cried suddenly, 'in the course of this fortnight I have come to know the value of a pure woman's heart, and my past seems further from me than ever.'

Lisa was confused, and she went gently into the flower-garden towards Lenotchka and Shurotchka.

'But I am glad I showed you that newspaper,' said Lavretsky, walking after her; 'already I have grown used to hiding nothing from you, and I hope you will repay me with the same confidence.'

'Do you expect it?' said Lisa, standing still. 'In that case I ought—but no! It is impossible.'

'What is it? Tell me, tell me.'

'Really, I believe I ought not—after all, though,' added Lisa, turning to Lavretsky with a smile, 'what's the good of half confidence? Do you know I received a letter to-day?'

'From Panshin?'

'Yes. How did you know?'

'He asks for your hand?'

'Yes,' replied Lisa, looking Lavretsky straight in the face with a serious expression.

Lavretsky on his side looked seriously at Lisa.

'Well, and what answer have you given him?' he managed to say at last.

'I don't know what answer to give,' replied Lisa, letting her clasped hands fall.

'How is that? Do you love him, then?'

'Yes, I like him; he seems a nice man.'

'You said the very same thing, and in the very same words, three days ago. I want to know do you love him with that intense passionate feeling which we usually call love?'

'As you understand it—no.'

'You're not in love with him'?

'No. But is that necessary?'

'What do you mean?'

'Mamma likes him,' continued Lisa, 'he is kind; I have nothing against him.'

'You hesitate, however.'

'Yes—and perhaps—you, your words are the cause of it. Do you remember what you said three days ago? But that is weakness.'

'O my child!' cried Lavretsky suddenly, and his voice was shaking, 'don't cheat yourself with sophistries, don't call weakness the cry of your heart, which is not ready to give itself without love. Do not take on yourself such a fearful responsibility to this man, whom you don't love, though you are ready to belong to him.'

'I'm obeying, I take nothing on myself,' Lisa was murmuring.

'Obey your heart; only that will tell you the truth,' Lavretsky interrupted her. 'Experience, prudence, all that is dust and ashes! Do not deprive yourself of the best, of the sole happiness on earth.'

'Do you say that, Fedor Ivanitch? You yourself married for love, and were you happy?'

Lavretsky threw up his arms.

'Ah, don't talk about me! You can't even understand all that a young, inexperienced, badly brought-up boy may mistake for love! Indeed though, after all, why should I be unfair

[94]

to myself? I told you just now that I had not had happiness. No! I was happy!'

'It seems to me, Fedor Ivanitch,' Lisa murmured in a low voice—when she did not agree with the person who she was talking to, she always dropped her voice; and now too she was deeply moved—'happiness on earth does not depend on ourselves.'

'On ourselves, ourselves, believe me' (he seized both her hands; Lisa grew pale and almost with terror but still steadfastly looked at him): 'if only we do not ruin our lives. For some people marriage for love may be unhappiness; but not for you, with your calm temperament, and your clear soul; I beseech you, do not marry without love, from a sense of duty, self-sacrifice, or anything. . . . That is infidelity, that is mercenary, and worse still. Believe me,—I have the right to say so; I have paid dearly for the right. And if your God——.'

At that instant Lavretsky noticed that Lenotchka and Shurotchka were standing near Lisa, and staring in dumb amazement at him. He dropped Lisa's hands, saying hurriedly, 'I beg your pardon,' and turned away towards the house.

'One thing only I beg of you,' he added, returning again to Lisa: 'don't decide at once, wait a little, think of what I have said to you. Even if you don't believe me, even if you did decide on a marriage of prudence—even in that case you mustn't marry Panshin. He can't be your husband. You will promise me not to be in a hurry, won't you?'

Lisa tried to answer Lavretsky, but she did not utter a word—not because she was resolved to 'be in a hurry', but because her heart was beating too violently and a feeling, akin to terror, stopped her breath.

* *30* *

As he was coming away from the Kalitins, Lavretsky met Panshin; they bowed coldly to one another. Lavretsky went to his lodgings, and locked himself in. He was experiencing emotions such as he had hardly ever experienced before. How long ago was it since he had thought himself in a state of peaceful petrifaction? How long was it since he had felt as he had expressed himself, at the very bottom of the river? What had changed his position? What had brought him out of his solitude? The most ordinary, inevitable, though always unexpected event, death? Yes; but he was not thinking so much of his wife's death and his own freedom, as of this question—what answer would Lisa give Panshin? He felt that in the course of the last three days, he had come to look at her with different eyes; he remembered how after returning home when he thought of her in the silence of the night, he had said to himself, 'if only!' . . . That 'if only'—in which he had referred to the past, to the impossible, had come to pass, though not as he had imagined it,—but his freedom alone was little. 'She will obey her mother,' he thought, 'she will marry Panshin; but even if she refuses him, won't it be just the same as far as I am concerned?' Going up to the looking-glass he minutely scrutinised his own face and shrugged his shoulders.

The day passed quickly by in these meditations; and evening came. Lavretsky went to the Kalitins'. He walked quickly, but his pace slackened as he drew near the house. Before the steps was standing Panshin's light carriage. 'Come,' thought Lavretsky, 'I will not be an egoist'—and he went into the house. He met with no one within-doors, and there was no sound in the drawing-room; he opened the door and saw Marya Dmitrievna playing picquet with Panshin. Panshin bowed to him without speaking, but the lady of the house cried, 'Well, this is unexpected!' and slightly frowned. Lavretsky sat down near her, and began to look at her cards.

'Do you know how to play picquet?' she asked him with a kind of hidden vexation, and then declared that she had thrown away a wrong card.

Panshin counted ninety, and began calmly and urbanely taking tricks with a severe and dignified expression of face. So it befits diplomatists to play; this was no doubt how he played in Petersburg with some influential dignitary, whom he wished to impress with a favourable opinion of his solidity and maturity. 'A hundred and one, a hundred and two, hearts, a hundred and three,' sounded his voice in measured tones, and Lavretsky could not decide whether it had a ring of reproach or of self-satisfaction.

'Can I see Marfa Timofyevna?' he inquired, observing that
Panshin was setting to work to shuffle the cards with still
more dignity. There was not a trace of the artist to be detected in him now.

'I think you can. She is at home, upstairs,' replied Marya
Dmitrievna; 'inquire for her.'

Lavretsky went up-stairs. He found Marfa Timofyevna also
at cards; she was playing old maid with Nastasya Karpovna.
Roska barked at him; but both the old ladies welcomed him
cordially. Marfa Timofyevna especially seemed in excellent
spirits.

'Ah! Fedya!' she began, 'pray sit down, my dear. We are
just finishing our game. Would you like some preserve?
Shurotchka, bring him a pot of strawberry. You don't want
any? Well, sit there; only you mustn't smoke; I can't bear
your tobacco, and it makes Matross sneeze.'

Lavretsky made haste to assure her that he had not the
least desire to smoke.

'Have you been down-stairs?' the old lady continued.
'Whom did you see there? Is Panshin still on view? Did you
see Lisa? No? She was meaning to come up here. And here she
is: speak of angels—'

Lisa came into the room, and she flushed when she saw
Lavretsky.

'I came in for a minute, Marfa Timofyevna,' she was
beginning.

'Why for a minute?' interposed the old lady. 'Why are you
always in such a hurry, you young people? You see I have a
visitor; talk to him a little, and entertain him.'

Lisa sat down on the edge of a chair; she raised her eyes to
Lavretsky—and felt that it was impossible not to let him know
how her interview with Panshin had ended. But how was she
to do it? She felt both awkward and ashamed. She had not long
known him, this man who rarely went to church, and took his
wife's death so calmly—and here was she, confiding all her
secrets to him . . . It was true he took an interest in her; she
herself trusted him and felt drawn to him; but all the same,
she was ashamed, as though a stranger had been into her pure,
maiden bower.

Marfa Timofyevna came to her assistance.

'Well, if you won't entertain him,' said Marfa Timofyevna, 'who will, poor fellow? I am too old for him, he is too clever for me, and for Nastasya Karpovna he's too old, it's only the quite young men she will look at.'

'How can I entertain Fedor Ivanitch?' said Lisa. 'If he likes, had I not better play him something on the piano?' she added irresolutely.

'Capital; you're my clever girl,' rejoined Marfa Timofyevna. 'Step down-stairs, my dears; when you have finished, come back: I have been made old maid, I don't like it, I want to have my revenge.'

Lisa got up. Lavretsky went after her. As she went down the staircase, Lisa stopped.

'They say truly,' she began, 'that people's hearts are full of contradictions. Your example ought to frighten me, to make me distrust marriage for love; but I——'

'You have refused him?' interrupted Lavretsky.

'No; but I have not consented either. I told him everything, everything I felt, and asked him to wait a little. Are you pleased with me?' she added with a swift smile—and with a light touch of her hand on the banister she ran down the stairs.

'What shall I play to you?' she asked, opening the piano.

'What you like,' answered Lavretsky as he sat down so that he could look at her.

Lisa began to play, and for a long while she did not lift her eyes from her fingers. She glanced at last at Lavretsky, and stopped short; his face seemed strange and beautiful to her.

'What is the matter with you?' she asked.

'Nothing,' he replied; 'I'm very happy; I'm glad of you, I'm glad to see you—go on.'

'It seems to me,' said Lisa a few moments later, 'that if he had really loved me, he would not have written that letter; he must have felt that I could not give him an answer now.'

'That is of no consequence,' observed Lavretsky, 'what is important is that you don't love him.'

'Stop, how can we talk like this? I keep thinking of your dead wife, and you frighten me.'

'Don't you think, Voldemar, that my Liseta plays charmingly?' Marya Dmitrievna was saying at that moment to Panshin.

'Yes,' answered Panshin, 'very charmingly.'

Marya Dmitrievna looked tenderly at her young partner, but the latter assumed a still more important and care-worn air and called fourteen kings.

<h1 style="text-align:center">* 31 *</h1>

Lavretsky was not a young man; he could not long delude himself as to the nature of the feeling inspired in him by Lisa; he was brought on that day to the final conviction that he loved her. This conviction did not give him any great pleasure. 'Have I really nothing better to do,' he thought, 'at thirty-five than to put my soul into a woman's keeping again? But Lisa is not like *her*; she would not demand degrading sacrifices from me: she would not tempt me away from my duties; she would herself incite me to hard honest work, and we would walk hand in hand towards a noble aim. Yes,' he concluded his reflections, 'that's all very fine, but the worst of it is that she does not in the least wish to walk hand in hand with me. She meant it when she said that I frightened her. But she doesn't love Panshin either—a poor consolation!'

Lavretsky went back to Vassilyevskoe, but he could not get through four days there—so dull it seemed to him. He was also in agonies of suspense; the news announced by M. Jules required confirmation, and he had received no letters of any kind. He returned to the town and spent an evening at the Kalitins'. He could easily see that Marya Dmitrievna had been set against him; but he succeeded in softening her a little, by losing fifteen roubles to her at picquet, and he spent nearly half an hour almost alone with Lisa in spite of the fact that her mother had advised her the previous evening not to be too intimate with a man *qui a un si grand ridicule*. He found a change in her; she had become, as it were, more thoughtful. She reproached him for his absence and asked him would he not go on the morrow to mass? (The next day was Sunday.)

'Do go,' she said before he had time to answer, 'we will pray together for the repose of her soul.' Then she added that she did not know how to act—she did not know whether she had the right to make Panshin wait any longer for her decision.

'Why so?' inquired Lavretsky.

'Because,' she said, 'I begin now to suspect what that decision will be.'

She declared that her head ached and went to her own room upstairs, hesitatingly holding out the tips of her fingers to Lavretsky.

The next day Lavretsky went to mass. Lisa was already in the church when he came in. She noticed him though she did not turn round towards him. She prayed fervently, her eyes were full of a calm light, calmly she bowed her head and lifted it again. He felt that she was praying for him too, and his heart was filled with a marvellous tenderness. He was happy and a little ashamed. The people reverently standing, the homely faces, the harmonious singing, the scent of incense, the long slanting gleams of light from the windows, the very darkness of the walls and arched roofs, all went to his heart. For long he had not been to church, for long he had not turned to God: even now he uttered no words of prayer—he did not even pray without words—but, at least, for a moment in all his mind, if not in his body, he bowed down and meekly humbled himself to earth. He remembered how, in his child-hood, he had always prayed in church until he had felt, as it were, a cool touch on his brow; that, he used to think then, is the guardian angel receiving me, laying on me the seal of grace. He glanced at Lisa. 'You brought me here,' he thought, 'touch me, touch my soul.' She was still praying calmly; her face seemed to him full of joy, and he was softened anew: he prayed for another soul, peace; for his own, forgiveness.

They met in the porch; she greeted him with glad and gracious seriousness. The sun brightly lighted up the young grass in the church-yard, and the striped dresses and kerchiefs of the women; the bells of the churches near were tinkling overhead; and the crows were cawing about the hedges. Lavretsky stood with uncovered head, a smile on his lips; the light breeze lifted his hair, and the ribbons of Lisa's hat. He put Lisa and Lenotchka who was with her into their carriage, divided all his money among the poor, and peacefully saun-tered home.

32

Painful days followed for Fedor Ivanitch. He found himself in a continual fever. Every morning he made for the post, and tore open letters and papers in agitation, and nowhere did he find anything which could confirm or disprove the fateful rumour. Sometimes he was disgusting to himself. 'What am I about,' he thought, 'waiting, like a vulture for blood, for certain news of my wife's death'? He went to the Kalitins' every day, but things had grown no easier for him there; the lady of the house was obviously sulky with him, and received him very condescendingly. Panshin treated him with exaggerated politeness; Lemm had entrenched himself in his misanthropy and hardly bowed to him, and, worst of all, Lisa seemed to avoid him. When she happened to be left alone with him, instead of her former candour there was visible embarrassment on her part, she did not know what to say to him, and he, too, felt confused. In the space of a few days Lisa had become quite different from what she was as he knew her: in her movements, her voice, her very laugh a secret tremor, an unevenness never there before was apparent. Marya Dmitrievna, like a true egoist, suspected nothing; but Marfa Timofyevna began to keep a watch over her favourite. Lavretsky more than once reproached himself for having shown Lisa the newspaper he had received; he could not but be conscious that in his spiritual condition there was something revolting to a pure nature. He imagined also that the change in Lisa was the result of her inward conflicts, her doubts as to what answer to give Panshin. One day she brought him a book, a novel of Walter Scott's, which she had herself asked him for.

'Have you read it?' he said.

'No; I can't bring myself to read just now,' she answered, and was about to go away.

'Stop a minute, it is so long since I have been alone with you. You seem to be afraid of me.'

'Yes.'

'Why so, pray?'

'I don't know.'

Lavretsky was silent.

'Tell me,' he began, 'you haven't yet decided?'

'What do you mean?' she said, not raising her eyes.

'You understand me.'

Lisa flushed crimson all at once.

'Don't ask me about anything!' she broke out hotly. 'I know nothing; I don't know myself.' And instantly she was gone.

The following day Lavretsky arrived at the Kalitins' after dinner and found there all the preparations for an evening service. In the corner of the dining-room on a square table covered with a clean cloth were already arranged, leaning up against the wall, the small holy pictures, in gold frames, set with tarnished jewels. The old servant in a grey coat and shoes was moving noiselessly and without haste all about the room; he set two wax-candles in the slim candlesticks before the holy pictures, crossed himself, bowed, and slowly went out. The unlighted drawing-room was empty. Lavretsky went into the dining-room and asked if it was someone's name-day.

In a whisper they told him no, but that the evening service had been arranged at the desire of Lisaveta Mihalovna and Marfa Timofyevna; that it had been intended to invite a wonder-working image, but that the latter had gone thirty *versts* away to visit a sick man. Soon the priest arrived with the deacons; he was a man no longer young, with a large bald head; he coughed loudly in the hall: the ladies at once filed slowly out of the boudoir, and went up to receive his blessing; Lavretsky bowed to them in silence; and in silence they bowed to him. The priest stood still for a little while, coughed once again, and asked in a bass undertone—

'You wish me to begin?'

'Pray begin, father,' replied Marya Dmitrievna.

He began to put on his robes; a deacon in a surplice asked obsequiously for a hot ember; there was a scent of incense. The maids and menservants came out from the hall, and remained huddled close together before the door. Roska, who never came down from up-stairs, suddenly ran into the dining-room; they began to chase her out; she was scared, doubled back into the room and sat down; a footman picked her up and carried her away.

The evening service began. Lavretsky squeezed himself into a corner; his emotions were strange, almost sad; he could not himself make out clearly what he was feeling. Marya Dmitrievna stood in front of all, before the chairs; she crossed herself with languid carelessness, like a grand lady, and first looked about her, then suddenly lifted her eyes to the ceiling; she was bored. Marfa Timofyevna looked worried; Nastasya Karpovna bowed down to the ground and got up with a kind of discreet, subdued rustle; Lisa remained standing in her place motionless; from the concentrated expression of her face it could be seen that she was praying steadfastly and fervently. When she bowed to the cross at the end of the service, she also kissed the large red hand of the priest. Marya Dmitrievna invited the latter to have some tea; he took off his vestment, assumed a somewhat more worldly air, and passed into the drawing-room with the ladies. Conversation—not too lively—began. The priest drank four cups of tea, incessantly wiping his bald head with his handkerchief; he related among other things that the merchant Avoshnikov was subscribing seven hundred roubles to gilding the *'cumpola'* of the church, and informed them of a sure remedy against freckles. Lavretsky tried to sit near Lisa, but her manner was severe, almost stern, and she did not once glance at him. She appeared intentionally not to observe him; a kind of cold, grave enthusiasm seemed to have taken possession of her. Lavretsky for some reason or other tried to smile and to say something amusing; but there was perplexity in his heart, and he went away at last in secret bewilderment. . . . He felt there was something in Lisa to which he could never penetrate.

Another time Lavretsky was sitting in the drawing-room listening to the sly but tedious gossip of Gedeonovsky, when suddenly, without himself knowing why, he turned round and caught a profound, attentive questioning look in Lisa's eyes. . . . It was bent on him, this enigmatic look. Lavretsky thought of it the whole night long. His love was not like a boy's; sighs and agonies were not in his line, and Lisa herself did not inspire a passion of that kind; but for every age love has its tortures—and he was spared none of them.

* 33 *

One day Lavretsky, according to his habit, was at the
Kalitins'. After an exhaustingly hot day, such a lovely evening
had set in that Marya Dmitrievna, in spite of her aversion to
a draught, ordered all the windows and doors into the garden
to be thrown open, and declared that she would not play cards,
that it was a sin to play cards in such weather, and one ought
to enjoy nature. Panshin was the only guest. He was stimu-
lated by the beauty of the evening, and conscious of a flood of
artistic sensations, but he did not care to sing before Lavretsky, so he fell to reading poetry; he read aloud well, but too
self-consciously and with unnecessary refinements, a few
poems of Lermontov (Pushkin had not then come into fashion
again). Then suddenly, as though ashamed of his enthusiasm,
began, *à propos* of the well-known poem, 'A Reverie', to
attack and fall foul of the younger generation. While doing
so he did not lose the opportunity of expounding how he
would change everything after his own fashion, if the power
were in his hands. 'Russia,' he said, 'has fallen behind Europe;
we must catch her up. It is maintained that we are young—
that's nonsense. Moreover we have no inventiveness: Homa-
kov himself admits that we have not even invented mouse-
traps. Consequently, whether we will or no, we must borrow
from others. We are sick, Lermontov says—I agree with him.
But we are sick from having only half become Europeans, we
must take a hair of the dog that bit us (*'le cadastre'*, thought
Lavretsky). 'The best heads, *les meilleures têtes,*' he continued,
'among us have long been convinced of it. All peoples are
essentially alike; only introduce among them good institutions,
and the thing is done. Of course there may be adaptation
to the existing national life; that is our affair—the affair of the
official (he almost said "governing") class. But in case of
need don't be uneasy. The institutions will transform the life
itself.' Marya Dmitrievna most feelingly assented to all Panshin said. 'What a clever man,' she thought, 'is talking in my
drawing-room!' Lisa sat in silence leaning back against the
window; Lavretsky too was silent. Marfa Timofyevna, playing cards with her old friend in the corner, muttered some-

thing to herself. Panshin walked up and down the room, and spoke eloquently, but with secret exasperation. It seemed as if he were abusing not a whole generation but a few people known to him. In a great lilac-bush in the Kalitins' garden a nightingale had built its nest; its first evening notes filled the pauses of the eloquent speech; the first stars were beginning to shine in the rosy sky over the motionless tops of the limes. Lavretsky got up and began to answer Panshin; an argument sprang up. Lavretsky championed the youth and the independence of Russia; he was ready to throw over himself and his generation, but he stood up for the new men, their convictions and desires. Panshin answered sharply and irritably. He maintained that the intelligent people ought to change everything, and was at last even brought to the point of forgetting his position as a *Kammeryunker*, and his career as an official, and calling Lavretsky an antiquated conservative, even hinting— very remotely it is true—at his dubious position in society. Lavretsky did not lose his temper. He did not raise his voice (he recollected that Mihalevitch too had called him antiquated but an antiquated Voltairean), and calmly proceeded to refute Panshin at all points. He proved to him the impracticability of sudden leaps and reforms from above, founded neither on knowledge of the mother-country, nor on any genuine faith in any ideal, even a negative one. He brought forward his own education as an example, and demanded before all things a recognition of the true spirit of the people and submission to it, without which even a courageous combat against error is impossible. Finally he admitted the reproach —well-deserved as he thought—of reckless waste of time and strength.

'That is all very fine!' cried Panshin at last, getting angry. 'You now have just returned to Russia, what do you intend to do?'

'Cultivate the soil,' answered Lavretsky, 'and try to cultivate it as well as possible.'

'That is very praiseworthy, no doubt,' rejoined Panshin, 'and I have been told that you have already had great success in that line; but you must allow that not everyone is fit for pursuits of that kind.'

'*Une nature poétique*,' observed Marya Dmitrievna, 'cannot, to be sure, cultivate . . . *et puis*, it is your vocation, Vladimir Nikolaitch, to do everything *en grand*.'

This was too much even for Panshin: he grew confused, and changed the conversation. He tried to turn it upon the beauty of the starlit sky, the music of Schubert; nothing was successful. He ended by proposing to Marya Dmitrievna a game of picquet. 'What! on such an evening?' she replied feebly. She ordered the cards to be brought in, however. Panshin tore open a new pack of cards with a loud crash, and Lisa and Lavretsky both got up as if by agreement, and went and placed themselves near Marfa Timofyevna. They both felt all at once so happy that they were even a little afraid of remaining alone together, and at the same time they both felt that the embarrassment they had been conscious of for the last few days had vanished, and would return no more. The old lady stealthily patted Lavretsky on the cheek, slyly screwed up her eyes, and shook her head once or twice, adding in a whisper, 'You have shut up our clever friend, many thanks.' Everything was hushed in the room; the only sound was the faint crackling of the wax-candles, and sometimes the tap of a hand on the table, and an exclamation or reckoning of points; and the rich torrent of the nightingale's song, powerful piercingly sweet, poured in at the window, together with the dewy freshness of the night.

✻ *34* ✻

Lisa had not uttered one word in the course of the dispute between Lavretsky and Panshin, but she had followed it attentively and was completely on Lavretsky's side. Politics interested her very little; but the supercilious tone of the worldly official (he had never delivered himself in that way before) repelled her; his contempt for Russia wounded her. It had never occurred to Lisa that she was a patriot; but her heart was with the Russian people; the Russian turn of mind delighted her; she would talk for hours together without ceremony to the peasant-overseer of her mother's property when he came to the town, and she talked to him as to an equal, without any of the condescension of a superior. Lavretsky felt all this; he would not have troubled himself to answer Panshin by himself; he had spoken only for Lisa's sake. They had said nothing to one another, their eyes even had seldom met. But they both knew that they had grown closer that evening, they knew that they liked and disliked the same things. On one point only were they divided; but Lisa secretly hoped to bring him to God. They sat near Marfa Timofyevna, and appeared to be following her play; indeed, they were really following it, but meanwhile their hearts were full, and nothing was lost on them; for them the nightingale sang, and the stars shone, and the trees gently murmured, lulled to sleep by the summer warmth and softness. Lavretsky was completely carried away, and surrendered himself wholly to his passion—and rejoiced in it. But no word can express what was passing in the pure heart of the young girl. It was a mystery for herself. Let it remain a mystery for all. No one knows, no one has seen, nor will ever see, how the grain, destined to life and growth, swells and ripens in the bosom of the earth.

Ten o'clock struck. Marfa Timofyevna went off up-stairs to her own apartments with Nastasya Karpovna. Lavretsky and Lisa walked across the room, stopped at the open door into the garden, looked into the darkness in the distance and then at one another, and smiled. They could have taken each other's hands, it seemed, and talked to their hearts' content. They returned to Marya Dmitrievna and Panshin, where a game of picquet was still dragging on. The last king was called at last, and the lady of the house rose, sighing and groaning from her well-cushioned easy-chair. Panshin took his hat, kissed Marya Dmitrievna's hand, remarking that nothing hindered some happy people now from sleeping, but that he had to sit up over stupid papers till morning, and departed, bowing coldly to Lisa (he had not expected that she would ask him to wait so long for an answer to his offer, and he was cross with her for it). Lavretsky followed him. They parted at the gate. Panshin waked his coachman by poking him in the neck with the end of his stick, took his seat in the carriage and rolled away. Lavretsky did not want to go home. He walked away from the town into the open country. The night was still and clear, though there was no moon. Lavretsky rambled a long time over the dewy grass. He came across a little narrow path; and went along it. It led him up to a long fence, and to a little gate; he tried, not knowing why, to push it open. With a faint creak the gate opened, as though it had been awaiting the touch of his hand. Lavretsky went into the garden. After a few paces along a walk of lime-trees he stopped short in amazement; he recognized the Kalitins' garden.

He moved at once into a black patch of shade thrown by a thick clump of hazels, and stood a long while without moving, shrugging his shoulders in astonishment.

'This cannot be for nothing,' he thought.

All was hushed around. From the direction of the house not a sound reached him. He went cautiously forward. At the bend of an avenue suddenly the whole house confronted him with its dark face; in two upstair-windows only a light was shining. In Lisa's room behind the white curtain a candle was burning, and in Marfa Timofyevna's bedroom a lamp shone with red-fire before the holy picture, and was reflected with equal brilliance on the gold frame. Below, the door on to the balcony gaped wide open. Lavretsky sat down on a wooden garden-seat, leaned on his elbows, and began to watch this door and Lisa's window. In the town it struck midnight; a little clock in the house shrilly clanged out twelve; the watchman beat it with jerky strokes upon his board. Lavretsky had no thought, no expectation; it was sweet to him to feel himself near Lisa, to sit in her garden on the seat where she herself had sat more than once.

The light in Lisa's room vanished.

'Sleep well, my sweet girl,' whispered Lavretsky, still sitting motionless, his eyes fixed on the darkened window.

Suddenly the light appeared in one of the windows of the ground-floor, then changed into another, and a third. . . . Someone was walking through the rooms with a candle. 'Can it be Lisa? It cannot be.' Lavretsky got up. . . . He caught a glimpse of a well-known face—Lisa came into the drawing-room. In a white gown, her plaits hanging loose on her shoulders, she went quietly up to the table, bent over it, put down the candle, and began looking for something. Then turning round facing the garden, she drew near the open door, and stood on the threshold, a light slender figure all in white. A shiver passed over Lavretsky.

'Lisa!' broke hardly audibly from his lips.

She started and began to gaze into the darkness.

'Lisa!' Lavretsky repeated louder, and he came out of the shadow of the avenue.

Lisa raised her head in alarm, and shrank back. She had recognised him. He called to her a third time, and stretched out his hands to her. She came away from the door and stepped into the garden.

'Is it you?' she said. 'You here?'

'I—I—listen to me,' whispered Lavretsky, and seizing her hand he led her to the seat.

She followed him without resistance, her pale face, her fixed eyes, and all her gestures expressed an unutterable bewilderment. Lavretsky made her sit down and stood before her.

'I did not mean to come here,' he began. 'Something brought me. . . . I—I love you,' he uttered in involuntary terror.

Lisa slowly looked at him. It seemed as though she only at that instant knew where she was and what was happening. She tried to get up, she could not, and she covered her face with her hands.

'Lisa,' murmured Lavretsky. 'Lisa,' he repeated, and fell at her feet.

Her shoulders began to heave slightly; the fingers of her pale hands were pressed more closely to her face.

'What is it?' Lavretsky urged, and he heard a subdued sob. His heart stood still. . . . He knew the meaning of those tears. 'Can it be that you love me?' he whispered, and caressed her knees.

'Get up', he heard her voice, 'get up, Fedor Ivanitch. What are we doing?'

He got up and sat beside her on the seat. She was not weeping now, and she looked at him steadfastly with her wet eyes.

'It frightens me: what are we doing?' she repeated.

'I love you,' he said again. 'I am ready to devote my whole life to you.'

She shuddered again, as though something had stung her, and lifted her eyes towards heaven.

'All that is in God's hands,' she said.

'But you love me, Lisa? We shall be happy.' She dropped her eyes; he softly drew her to him, and her head sank on to his shoulder. . . . He bent his head a little and touched her pale lips.

Half an hour later Lavretsky was standing before the little garden gate. He found it locked and was obliged to get over the fence. He returned to the town and walked along the slumbering streets. A sense of immense, unhoped-for happiness filled his soul; all his doubts had died away. 'Away, dark phantom of the past,' he thought. 'She loves me, she will be mine.' Suddenly it seemed to him that in the air over his head were floating strains of divine triumphant music. He stood still. The music resounded in still greater magnificence; a mighty flood of melody—and all his bliss seemed speaking and singing in its strains. He looked about him; the music floated down from two upper windows of a small house.

'Lemm?' cried Lavretsky as he ran to the house. 'Lemm! Lemm!' he repeated aloud.

The sounds died away and the figure of the old man in a dressing-gown, with his throat bare and his hair dishevelled, appeared at the window.

'Aha!' he said with dignity, 'is it you'?

'Christopher Fedoritch, what marvellous music! for mercy's sake, let me in.'

Without uttering a word, the old man with a majestic flourish of the arm dropped the key of the street door from the window.

Lavretsky hastened up-stairs, went into the room and was about to rush up to Lemm; but the latter imperiously motioned him to a seat, saying abruptly in Russian, 'Sit down and listen,' sat down himself to the piano, and looking proudly and severely about him, he began to play. It was long since Lavretsky had listened to anything like it. The sweet passionate melody went to his heart from the first note; it was glowing and languishing with inspiration, happiness and beauty; it swelled and melted away; it touched on all that is precious, mysterious, and holy on earth. It breathed of deathless sorrow and mounted dying away to the heavens. Lavretsky drew himself up, and rose cold and pale with ecstasy. This music seemed to clutch his very soul, so lately shaken by the rapture of love, the music was glowing with love too. 'Again!' he whispered as the last chord sounded. The old man threw him an eagle glance, struck his hand on his chest and saying deliberately in his own tongue, 'This is my work, I am a great musician,' he played again his marvellous composition. There was no candle in the room; the light of the rising moon fell aslant on the window; the soft air was vibrating with sound; the poor little room seemed a holy place, and the old man's head stood out noble and inspired in the silvery half light. Lavretsky went up to him and embraced him. At first Lemm did not respond to his embrace, and even pushed him away with his elbow. For a long time without moving in any limb he kept the same severe, almost morose expression, and only growled out twice, 'aha'. At last his face relaxed, changed, and grew calmer, and in response to Lavretsky's warm congratulations he smiled a little at first, then burst into tears, and sobbed weakly like a child.

'It is wonderful,' he said, 'that you have come just at this moment; but I know all, I know all.'

'You know all?' Lavretsky repeated in amazement.

'You have heard me,' replied Lemm, 'did you not understand that I knew all?'

Till daybreak Lavretsky could not sleep; all night he was sitting on his bed. And Lisa too did not sleep; she was praying.

* *35* *

The reader knows how Lavretsky grew up and developed. Let us say a few words about Lisa's education. She was in her tenth year when her father died; but he had not troubled himself much about her. Weighed down with business cares, for ever anxious for the increase of his property, bilious, sharp and impatient, he gave money unsparingly for the teachers, tutors, dress and other necessities of his children; but he could not endure, as he expressed it, 'to be dandling his squallers', and indeed he had no time to dandle them. He worked, took no rest from business, slept little, rarely played cards, and worked again. He compared himself to a horse harnessed to a threshing-machine. 'My life has soon come to an end,' was his comment on his death-bed, with a bitter smile on his parched lips. Marya Dmitrievna did not in reality trouble herself about Lisa any more than her husband, though she had boasted to Lavretsky that she alone had educated her children. She dressed her up like a doll, stroked her on the head before visitors and called her a clever child and a darling to her face, and that was all. Any kind of continuous care was too exhausting for the indolent lady. During her father's lifetime, Lisa was in the hands of a governess, Mademoiselle Moreau from Paris; after his death she passed into the charge of Marfa Timofyevna. Marfa Timofyevna the reader knows already; Mademoiselle Moreau was a tiny wrinkled creature with little bird-like ways and a bird's intellect. In her youth she had led a very dissipated life, but in old age she had only two passions left—gluttony and cards. When she had eaten her fill, and was neither playing cards nor chattering, her face assumed an expression almost death-like. She was sitting, looking, breathing—yet it was clear that there was not an idea in her head. One could not even call her good-natured. Birds are not good-natured. Either as a result of her frivolous youth or of the air of Paris, which she had breathed from childhood, a kind of cheap universal scepticism had found its way into her, usually expressed by the words: *tout ça c'est des bêtises.* She spoke ungrammatically, but in pure Parisian jargon, did not talk scandal and had no caprices—what more can one desire in a governess? Over Lisa she had little influence; all the stronger was the influence on her of her nurse, Agafya Vlasyevna.

This women's story was remarkable. She came of a peasant family. She was married at sixteen to a peasant; but she was strikingly different from her peasant sisters. Her father had been twenty years *starosta*, and had made a good deal of money, and he spoiled her. She was exceptionally beautiful, the best-dressed girl in the whole district, clever, ready with her tongue, and daring. Her master Dmitri Pestov, Marya Dmitrievna's father, a man of modest and gentle character, saw her one day at the threshing-floor, talked to her and fell passionately in love with her. She was soon left a widow; Pestov, though he was a married man, took her into his house and dressed her like a lady. Agafya at once adapted herself to her new position, just as if she had never lived differently all her life. She grew fairer and plumper; her arms grew as 'floury white' under her muslin-sleeves as a merchant's lady's; the samovar never left her table; she would wear nothing except silk or velvet, and slept on well-stuffed feather-beds. This blissful existence lasted for five years, but Dimitri Pestov died; his widow, a kind-hearted woman, out of regard for the memory of the deceased, did not wish to treat her rival unfairly, all the more because Agafya had never forgotten herself in her presence. She married her, however, to a shepherd, and sent her a long way off. Three years passed. It happened one hot summer day that her mistress in driving past stopped at the cattle-yard. Agafya regaled her with such delicious cool cream, behaved so modestly, and was so neat, so bright, and so contented with everything that her mistress signified her forgiveness to her and allowed her to return to the house. Within six months she had become so much attached to her that she raised her to be housekeeper, and intrusted the whole household management to her. Agafya again returned to power, and again grew plump and fair; her mistress put the most complete confidence in her. So passed five years more. Misfortune again overtook Agafya. Her husband, whom she had promoted to be a footman, began to drink, took to vanishing from the house, and ended by stealing six of the mistress' silver spoons and hiding them till a favourable moment in his wife's box. It was opened. He was sent to be a shepherd again, and Agafya fell into disgrace. She was not turned out of the house, but was degraded from housekeeper to being a sewing-woman and was ordered to wear a kerchief on her head instead of a cap. To the astonishment of everyone, Agafya accepted with humble resignation the blow that had fallen upon her. She was at that time about thirty, all her children were dead and her husband did not live much longer. The time had come for her to reflect. And she did reflect. She became very silent and devout, never missed a single matin's service nor a single mass, and gave away all her fine clothes. She spent fifteen years quietly, peacefully, and soberly, never quarrelling with any one and giving way to everyone. If any one scolded her, she only bowed to them and thanked them for the admonition. Her mistress had long ago forgiven her, raised her out of disgrace, and had made her a present of a cap of her own. But she was herself unwilling to give up the kerchief and always wore a dark dress. After her mistress' death she became still more quiet and humble. A Russian readily feels fear, and affection; but it is hard to gain his respect: it is not soon given, nor to everyone. For Agafya everyone in the house had great respect; no one even remembered her previous sins, as though they had been buried with the old master.

When Kalitin became Marya Dmitrievna's husband, he wanted to intrust the care of the house to Agafya. But she refused 'on account of temptation'; he scolded her, but she bowed humbly and left the room. Kalitin was clever in understanding men; he understood Agafya and did not forget her. When he moved to the town, he gave her, with her consent, the place of nurse to Lisa, who was only just five years old.

Lisa was at first frightened by the austere and serious face of her new nurse; but she soon grew used to her and began to love her. She was herself a serious child. Her features recalled Kalitin's decided and regular profile, only her eyes were not her father's; they were lighted up by a gentle attentiveness and goodness, rare in children. She did not care to play with dolls, never laughed loudly or for long, and behaved with great decorum. She was not often thoughtful, but when she was, it was almost always with some reason. After a short silence, she usually turned to some grown-up person with a question which showed that her brain had been at work upon some new impression. She very early got over childish lispings, and by the time she was four years old spoke perfectly plainly. She was afraid of her father; her feeling towards her mother was undefinable, she was not afraid of her, nor was she demonstrative to her; but she was not demonstrative even towards Agafya, though she was the only person she loved. Agafya never left her. It was curious to see them together. Agafya, all in black, with a dark handkerchief on her head, her face thin and transparent as wax, but still beautiful and expressive, would be sitting upright, knitting a stocking; Lisa would sit at her feet in a little arm-chair, also busied over some kind of work, and seriously raising her clear eyes, listening to what Agafya was relating to her. And Agafya did not tell her stories; but in even measured accents she would narrate the life of the Holy Virgin, the lives of hermits, saints, and holy men. She would tell Lisa how the holy men lived in deserts, how they were saved, how they suffered hunger and want, and did not fear kings, but confessed Christ; how fowls of the air brought them food and wild beasts listened to them, and flowers sprang up on the spots where their blood had been spilt. 'Wallflowers?' asked Lisa one day, she was very fond of flowers. . . . Agafya spoke to Lisa gravely and meekly, as though she felt herself to be unworthy to utter such high and holy words. Lisa listened to her, and the image of the all-seeing, all-knowing God penetrated with a kind of sweet power into her very soul, filling it with pure and reverent awe; but Christ became for her something near, well-known, almost familiar. Agafya taught her to pray also. Sometimes she wakened Lisa early at daybreak, dressed her hurriedly, and took her in secret to matins. Lisa followed her on tiptoe, almost holding her breath. The cold and twilight of the early morning, the freshness and emptiness of the church, the very secrecy of these unexpected expeditions, the cautious return home and to her little bed, all these mingled impressions of the forbidden, strange, and holy agitated the little girl and penetrated to the very innermost depths of her nature. Agafya never censured any one, and never scolded Lisa for being naughty. When she was displeased at anything, she only kept silence. And Lisa understood this silence; with a child's quick-sightedness she knew very well, too, when Agafya was displeased with other people, Marya Dmitrievna, or Kalitin himself. For a little over three years Agafya waited on Lisa, then Mademoiselle

Moreau replaced her; but the frivolous Frenchwoman, with her cold ways and exclamation, *tout ça c'est des bêtises*, could never dislodge her dear nurse from Lisa's heart; the seeds that had been dropped into it had become too deeply rooted. Besides, though Agafya no longer waited on Lisa, she was still in the house and often saw her charge, who believed in her as before.

Agafya did not, however, get on well with Marfa Timofyevna, when she came to live in the Kalitin's house. Such gravity and dignity on the part of one who had once worn the motley skirt of a peasant wench displeased the impatient and self-willed old lady. Agafya asked leave to go on a pilgrimage and she never came back. There were dark rumours that she had gone off to a retreat of sectaries. But the impression she had left in Lisa's soul was never obliterated. She went as before to the mass as to a festival, she prayed with rapture, with a kind of restrained and shamefaced transport, at which Marya Dmitrievna secretly marvelled not a little, and even Marfa Timofyevna, though she did not restrain Lisa in any way, tried to temper her zeal, and would not let her make too many prostrations to the earth in her prayers; it was not a lady-like habit, she would say. In her studies Lisa worked well, that is to say perseveringly; she was not gifted with specially brilliant abilities, or great intellect; she could not succeed in anything without labour. She played the piano well, but only Lemm knew what it had cost her. She had read little; she had not 'words of her own', but she had her own ideas, and she went her own way. It was not only on the surface that she took after her father; he, too, had never asked other people what was to be done. So she had grown up tranquilly and restfully till she had reached the age of nineteen. She was very charming, without being aware of it herself. Her every movement was full of spontaneous, somewhat awkward gracefulness; her voice had the silvery ring of untouched youth, the least feeling of pleasure called forth an enchanting smile on her lips, and added a deep light and a kind of mystic sweetness to her kindling eyes. Penetrated through and through by a sense of duty, by the dread of hurting any one whatever, with a kind and tender heart, she had loved all men, and no one in particular; God only she had

loved passionately, timidly, and tenderly. Lavretsky was the
first to break in upon her peaceful inner life.

Such was Lisa.

* *36* *

On the following day at twelve o'clock, Lavretsky set off
to the Kalitins. On the way he met Panshin, who galloped
past him on horseback, his hat pulled down to his very eyebrows. At the Kalitins', Lavretsky was not admitted for the
first time since he had been acquainted with them. Marya
Dmitrievna was 'resting', so the footman informed him; her
excellency had a headache. Marfa Timofyevna and Lisaveta
Mihalovna were not at home. Lavretsky walked round the
garden in the faint hope of meeting Lisa, but he saw no one.
He came back two hours later and received the same answer,
accompanied by a rather dubious look from the footman.
Lavretsky thought it would be unseemly to call for a third
time the same day, and he decided to drive over to Vassilyevskoe, where he had business moreover. On the road he
made various plans for the future, each better than the last;
but he was overtaken by a melancholy mood when he reached
his aunt's little village. He fell into conversation with Anton;
the old man, as if purposely, seemed full of cheerless fancies.
He told Lavretsky how, at her death, Glafira Petrovna had
bitten her own arm, and after a brief pause, added with a
sigh: 'Every man, dear master, is destined to devour himself.' It was late when Lavretsky set off on the way back. He
was haunted by the music of the day before, and Lisa's image
returned to him in all its sweet distinctness; he mused with
melting tenderness over the thought that she loved him, and
reached his little house in the town, soothed and happy.

The first thing that struck him as he went into the entrance hall was a scent of patchouli, always distasteful to
him; there were some high travelling-trunks standing there.
The face of his groom, who ran out to meet him, seemed
strange to him. Not stopping to analyse his impressions, he
crossed the threshold of the drawing-room. . . . On his

entrance there rose from the sofa a lady in a black silk dress with flounces, who, raising a cambric handkerchief to her pale face, made a few paces forward, bent her carefully dressed, perfumed head, and fell at his feet. . . . Then, only, he recognised her: this lady was his wife!

He caught his breath. . . . He leaned against the wall.

'*Théodore*, do not repulse me!' she said in French, and her voice cut to his heart like a knife.

He looked at her senselessly, and yet he noticed involuntarily at once that she had grown both whiter and fatter.

'*Théodore*!' she went on, from time to time lifting her eyes and discreetly wringing her marvellously-beautiful fingers with their rosy, polished nails. '*Théodore*, I have wronged you, deeply wronged you; I will say more, I have sinned; but hear me; I am tortured by remorse, I have grown hateful to myself, I could endure my position no longer; how many times have I thought of turning to you, but I feared your anger; I resolved to break every tie with the past. . . . *Puis, j'ai été si malade.* . . . I have been so ill,' she added, and passed her hand over her brow and cheek. 'I took advantage of the widely-spread rumour of my death, I gave up everything; without resting day or night I hastened hither; I hesitated long to appear before you, my judge . . . *paraître devant vous, mon juge*; but I was resolved at last, remembering your constant goodness, to come to you; I found your address at Moscow. Believe me,' she went on, slowly getting up from the floor and sitting on the very edge of an arm-chair, 'I have often thought of death, and I should have found courage enough to take my life . . . ah! life is a burden unbearable for me now! . . . but the thought of my daughter, my little Ada, stopped me. She is here, she is asleep in the next room, the poor child! She is tired—you shall see her; she at least has done you no wrong, and I am so unhappy, so unhappy!' cried Madame Lavretsky, and she melted into tears.

Lavretsky came to himself at last; he moved away from the wall and turned towards the door.

'You are going?' cried his wife in a voice of despair. 'Oh, this is cruel! Without uttering one word to me, not even a reproach. This contempt will kill me, it is terrible!'

Lavretsky stood still.

'What do you want to hear from me?' he articulated in an expressionless voice.

'Nothing, nothing,' she rejoined quickly, 'I know I have no right to expect anything; I am not mad, believe me; I do not hope, I do not dare to hope for your forgiveness; I only venture to entreat you to command me what I am to do, where I am to live. Like a slave I will fulfil your commands whatever they may be.'

'I have no commands to give you,' replied Lavretsky in the same colourless voice; 'you know, all is over between us . . . and now more than ever; you can live where you like; and if your allowance is too little——'

'Ah, don't say such dreadful things,' Varvara Pavlovna interrupted him, 'spare me, if only . . . if only for the sake of this angel.' And as she uttered these words, Varvara Pavlovna ran impulsively into the next room, and returned at once with a small and very elegantly dressed little girl in her arms. Thick flaxen curls fell over her pretty rosy little face, and on to her large sleepy black eyes; she smiled and blinked her eyes at the light and laid a chubby little hand on her mother's neck.

'*Ada, vois, c'est ton père,*' said Varvara Pavlovna, pushing the curls back from her eyes and kissing her vigorously, '*prie le avec moi.*'

'*C'est ça, papa?*' stammered the little girl lisping.

'*Oui, mon enfant, n'est-ce pas que tu l'aimes?*'

But this was more than Lavretsky could stand.

'In such a melodrama must there really be a scene like this?' he muttered, and went out of the room.

Varvara Pavlovna stood still for some time in the same place, slightly shrugged her shoulders, carried the little girl off into the next room, undressed her and put her to bed. Then she took up a book and sat down near the lamp, and after staying up for an hour she went to bed herself.

'*Eh bien, madame?*' queried her maid, a Frenchwoman whom she had brought from Paris, as she unlaced her corset.

'*En bien, Justine,*' she replied, 'he is a good deal older, but I fancy he is just the same good-natured fellow. Give me my gloves for the night, and get out my grey high-necked dress for tomorrow, and don't forget the mutton cutlets for Ada. . . .

I daresay it will be difficult to get them here; but we must try.'

'*A la guerre comme à la guerre*,' replied Justine, as she put out the candle.

* *37* *

For more than two hours Lavretsky wandered about the streets of the town. The night he had spent in the outskirts of Paris returned to his mind. His heart was bursting and his head, dull and stunned, was filled again with the same dark senseless angry thoughts, constantly recurring. 'She is alive, she is here,' he muttered, with ever fresh amazement. He felt that he had lost Lisa. His wrath choked him; this blow had fallen too suddenly upon him. How could he so readily have believed in the nonsensical gossip of a journal, a wretched scrap of paper? 'Well, if I had not believed it,' he thought, 'what difference would it have made? I should not have known that Lisa loved me; she would not have known it herself.' He could not rid himself of the image, the voice, the eyes of his wife . . . and he cursed himself, he cursed everything in the world.

Wearied out he went towards morning to Lemm's. For a long while he could make no one hear; at last at a window the old man's head appeared in a nightcap, sour, wrinkled, and utterly unlike the inspired austere visage which twenty-four hours before had looked down imperiously upon Lavretsky in all the dignity of artistic grandeur.

'What do you want?' queried Lemm. 'I can't play to you every night, I have taken a decoction for a cold.' But Lavretsky's face, apparently, struck him as strange; the old man made a shade for his eyes with his hand, took a look at his belated visitor, and let him in.

Lavretsky went into the room and sank into a chair. The old man stood still before him, wrapping the skirts of his shabby striped dressing-gown around him, shrinking together and gnawing his lips.

'My wife is here,' Lavretsky brought out. He raised his head and suddenly broke into involuntary laughter.

Lemm's face expressed bewilderment, but he did not even smile, only wrapped himself closer in his dressing-gown.

'Of course, you don't know,' Lavretsky went on, 'I had imagined . . . I read in a paper that she was dead.'

'O—oh, did you read that lately?' asked Lemm.

'Yes, lately.'

'O—oh,' repeated the old man, raising his eyebrows. 'And she is here?'

'Yes. She is at my house now; and I . . . I am an unlucky fellow.'

And he laughed again.

'You are an unlucky fellow,' Lemm repeated slowly.

'Christopher Fedoritch,' began Lavretsky, 'would you undertake to carry a note for me?'

'H'm. May I know to whom?'

'Lisavet——'

'Ah . . . yes, yes, I understand. Very good. And when must the letter be received?'

'Tomorrow, as early as possible.'

'H'm. I can send Katrine, my cook. No, I will go myself.'

'And you will bring me an answer?'

'Yes, I will bring an answer.'

Lemm sighed.

'Yes, my poor young friend; you are certainly an unlucky young man.'

Lavretsky wrote a few words to Lisa. He told her of his wife's arrival, begged her to appoint a meeting with him— then he flung himself on the narrow sofa, with his face to the wall; and the old man lay down on the bed, and kept muttering a long while, coughing and drinking off his decoction by gulps.

The morning came; they both got up. With strange eyes they looked at one another. At that moment Lavretsky longed to kill himself. The cook, Katrine, brought them some villainous coffee. It struck eight. Lemm put on his hat, and saying that he was going to give a lesson at the Kalitins' at ten, but he could find a suitable pretext for going there now, he set off. Lavretsky flung himself again on the little sofa, and once more the same bitter laugh stirred in the depth of his soul. He thought of how his wife had driven him out of his house; he imagined Lisa's position, covered his eyes and clasped his hands behind his head. At last Lemm came back and brought him a scrap of paper, on which Lisa had scribbled in pencil the following words: 'We cannot meet today; perhaps, tomorrow evening. Good-bye.' Lavretsky thanked Lemm briefly and indifferently, and went home.

He found his wife at breakfast; Ada, in curl-papers, in a little white frock with blue ribbons, was eating her mutton cutlet. Varvara Pavlovna rose at once directly Lavretsky entered the room, and went to meet him with humility in her face. He asked her to follow him into the study, shut the door after them, and began to walk up and down; she sat down, modestly laying one hand over the other, and began to follow his movements with her eyes, which were still beautiful, though they were pencilled lightly under their lids.

For some time Lavretsky could not speak; he felt that he could not master himself, he saw clearly that Varvara Pavlovna was not in the least afraid of him, but was assuming an appearance of being ready to faint away in another instant.

'Listen, madam,' he began at last, breathing with difficulty and at moments setting his teeth: 'it is useless for us to make pretences with one another; I don't believe in your penitence; and even if it were sincere, to be with you again, to live with you, would be impossible for me.'

Varvara Pavlovna bit her lips and half-closed her eyes. 'It is aversion,' she thought; 'all is over; in his eyes I am not even a woman.'

'Impossible,' repeated Lavretsky, fastening the top buttons of his coat. 'I don't know what induced you to come here; I suppose you have come to the end of your money.'

'Ah! you hurt me!' whispered Varvara Pavlovna.

'However that may be—you are, any way, my wife, unhappily. I cannot drive you away . . . and this is the proposal I make you. You may today, if you like, set off to Lavriky, and live there; there is, as you know, a good house there; you will have everything you need in addition to your allowance . . . Do you agree?'—Varvara Pavlovna raised an embroidered handkerchief to her face.

'I have told you already,' she said, her lips twitching nervously, 'that I will consent to whatever you think fit to do with me; at present it only remains for me to beg of you—will you allow me at least to thank you for your magnanimity?'

'No thanks, I beg—it is better without that,' Lavretsky said hurriedly. 'So then,' he pursued, approaching the door, 'I may reckon on——'

'Tomorrow I will be at Lavriky,' Varvara Pavlovna declared, rising respectfully from her place. 'But Fedor Ivanitch——' (She no longer called him '*Théodore*'.)

'What do you want?'

'I know, I have not yet gained any right to forgiveness; may I hope at least that with time——'

'Ah, Varvara Pavlovna,' Lavretsky broke in, 'you are a clever woman, but I too am not a fool; I know that you don't want forgiveness in the least. And I have forgiven you long ago; but there was always a great gulf between us.'

'I know how to submit,' rejoined Varvara Pavlovna, bowing her head. 'I have not forgotten my sin; I should not have been surprised if I had learnt that you even rejoiced at the news of my death,' she added softly, slightly pointing with her hand to the copy of the journal which was lying forgotten by Lavretsky on the table.

Fedor Ivanitch started; the paper had been marked in pencil. Varvara Pavlovna gazed at him with still greater humility. She was superb at that moment. Her grey Parisian gown clung gracefully round her supple, almost girlish figure; her slender, soft neck, encircled by a white collar, her bosom gently stirred by her even breathing, her hands innocent of bracelets and rings—her whole figure, from her shining hair to the tip of her just visible little shoe, was so artistic . . .

Lavretsky took her in with a glance of hatred; scarcely could he refrain from crying: 'Bravo!' scarcely could he refrain from felling her with a blow of his fist on her shapely head—and he turned on his heel. An hour later he had started for Vassilyevskoe, and two hours later Varvara Pavlovna had bespoken the best carriage in the town, had put on a simple straw hat with a black veil, and a modest mantle, given Ada into the charge of Justine, and set off to the Kalitins'. From the inquiries she had made among the servants, she had learnt that her husband went to see them every day.

∗ *38* ∗

The day of the arrival of Lavretsky's wife at the town of O——, a sorrowful day for him, had been also a day of misery for Lisa. She had not had time to go downstairs and say good-morning to her mother, when the tramp of hoofs was heard under the window, and with secret dismay she saw Panshin riding into the courtyard. 'He has come so early for a final explanation,' she thought, and she was not mistaken. After a turn in the drawing-room, he suggested that she should go with him into the garden, and then asked her for the decision of his fate. Lisa summoned up all her courage and told him that she could not be his wife. He heard her to the end, standing on one side of her and pulling his hat down over his forehead; courteously, but in a changed voice, he asked her, 'Was this her last word, and had he given her any ground for such a change in her views?'—then pressed his hand to his eyes, sighed softly and abruptly, and took his hand away from his face again.

'I did not want to go along the beaten track,' he said huskily. 'I wanted to choose a wife according to the dictates of my heart; but it seems this was not to be. Farewell, fond dream!' He made Lisa a profound bow, and went back into the house.

She hoped that he would go away at once; but he went into Marya Dmitrievna's room and remained nearly an hour with her. As he came out, he said to Lisa: '*Votre mère vous appelle; adieu à jamais,*' . . . mounted his horse and set off at full trot from the very steps. Lisa went in to Marya Dmitrievna and found her in tears; Panshin had informed her of his ill-luck.

'Do you want to be the death of me? Do you want to be the death of me?' was how the disconsolate widow began her lamentations. 'Whom do you want? Wasn't he good enough for you? A *Kammerjunker*! not interesting! He might have married any Maid of Honour he liked in Petersburg. And I—

I had so hoped for it! Is it long that you have changed towards him? How has this misfortune come on us—it cannot have come of itself! Is it that dolt of a cousin's doing? A nice person you have picked up to advise you!'

'And he, poor darling,' Marya Dmitrievna went on, 'how respectful he is, how attentive even in his sorrow! He has promised not to desert me. Ah, I can never bear that! Ah, my head aches fit to split! Send me Palashka. You will be the death of me, if you don't think better of it—do you hear?' And, calling her twice an ungrateful girl, Marya Dmitrievna dismissed her.

She went to her own room. But she had not had time to recover from her interviews with Panshin and her mother before another storm broke over her head, and this time from a quarter from which she would least have expected it. Marfa Timofyevna came into her room, and at once slammed the door after her. The old lady's face was pale, her cap was awry, her eyes were flashing, and her hands and lips were trembling. Lisa was astonished; she had never before seen her sensible and reasonable aunt in such a condition.

'A pretty thing, miss,' Marfa Timofyevna began in a shaking and broken whisper, 'a pretty thing! Who taught you such ways, I should like to know, miss? . . . Give me some water; I can't speak.'

'Calm yourself, auntie, what is the matter?' said Lisa, giving her a glass of water. 'Why, I thought you did not think much of Mr Panshin yourself.'

Marfa Timofyevna pushed away the glass.

'I can't drink; I shall knock my last teeth out it I try to. What's Panshin to do with it? Why bring Panshin in? You had better tell me who has taught you to make appointments at night—eh? miss?'

Lisa turned pale.

'Now, please, don't try to deny it,' pursued Marfa Timofyevna; 'Shurotchka herself saw it all and told me. I have had to forbid her chattering, but she is not a liar.'

'I don't deny it, auntie,' Lisa uttered scarcely audibly.

'Ah, ah! That's it, is it, miss; you made an appointment with him, that old sinner, who seems so meek?'

'No.'

'How then?'

'I went down into the drawing-room for a book; he was in the garden—and he called me.'

'And you went? A pretty thing! So you love him, eh?'

'I love him,' answered Lisa softly.

'Merciful Heavens! She loves him!' Marfa Timofyevna snatched off her cap. 'She loves a married man! Ah! she loves him.'

'He told me' . . . began Lisa.

'What has he told you, the scoundrel, eh?'

'He told me that his wife was dead.'

Marfa Timofyevna crossed herself. 'Peace be with her,' she muttered; 'she was a vain hussy, God forgive her. So, then, he's a widower, I suppose. And he's losing no time, I see. He has buried one wife and now he's after another. He's a nice person: only let me tell you one thing, niece; in my day, when I was young, harm came to young girls from such goings on. Don't be angry with me, my girl, only fools are angry at the truth. I have given orders not to admit him today. I love him, but I shall never forgive him for this. Upon my word, a widower! Give me some water. But as for your sending Panshin about his business, I think you're a first-rate girl for that. Only don't you go sitting of nights with any animals of that sort; don't break my old heart, or else you'll see I'm not all fondness—I can bite too . . . a widower!'

Marfa Timofyevna went off, and Lisa sat down in a corner and began to cry. There was bitterness in her soul. She had not deserved such humiliation. Love had proved no happiness to her: she was weeping for a second time since yesterday evening. This new unexpected feeling had only just arisen in her heart, and already what a heavy price she had paid for it, how coarsely had strange hands touched her sacred secret. She felt ashamed, and bitter, and sick; but she had no doubt and no dread—and Lavretsky was dearer to her than ever. She had hesitated while she did not understand herself; but after that meeting, after that kiss—she could hesitate no more: she knew that she loved, and now she loved honestly and seriously, she was bound firmly for all her life, and she did not fear reproaches. She felt that by no violence could they break that bond.

Marya Dmitrievna was much agitated when she received the announcement of the arrival of Varvara Pavlovna Lavretsky, she did not even know whether to receive her; she was afraid of giving offence to Fedor Ivanitch. At last curiosity prevailed. 'Why,' she reflected, 'she too is a relation,' and, taking up her position in an arm-chair, she said to the footman, 'Show her in.' A few moments passed; the door opened; Varvara Pavlovna, swiftly and with scarcely audible steps, approached Marya Dmitrievna, and not allowing her to rise from her chair, bent almost on her knees before her.

'I thank you, dear aunt,' she began in a soft voice full of emotion, speaking Russian; 'I thank you; I did not hope for such condescension on your part; you are an angel of goodness.'

As she uttered these words Varvara Pavlovna quite unexpectedly took possession of one of Mary Dmitrievna's hands, and pressing it lightly in her pale lavender gloves, she raised it in a fawning way to her full rosy lips. Marya Dmitrievna quite lost her head, seeing such a handsome and charmingly dressed woman almost at her feet. She did not know where she was. And she tried to withdraw her hand, while, at the same time, she was inclined to make her sit down, and to say something affectionate to her. She ended by raising Varvara Pavlovna and kissing her on her smooth perfumed brow. Varvara Pavlovna was completely overcome by this kiss.

'How do you do, *bonjour*,' said Marya Dmitrievna. 'Of course I did not expect . . . but, of course, I am glad to see you. You understand, my dear, it's not for me to judge between man and wife' . . .

'My husband is in the right in everything,' Varvara Pavlovna interposed; 'I alone am to blame.'

'That is a very praiseworthy feeling,' rejoined Marya Dmitrievna, 'very. Have you been here long? Have you seen him? But sit down, please.'

'I arrived yesterday,' answered Varvara Pavlovna, sitting down meekly. 'I have seen Fedor Ivanitch; I have talked with him.'

'Ah! Well, and how was he?'

'I was afraid my sudden arrival would provoke his anger,' continued Varvara Pavlovna, 'but he did not refuse to see me.'

'That is to say, he did not . . . Yes, yes, I understand,' commented Marya Dmitrievna, 'He is only a little rough on the surface, but his heart is soft.'

'Fedor Ivanitch has not forgiven me; he would not hear me. But he was so good as to assign me Lavriky as a place of residence.'

'Ah! a splendid estate!'

'I am setting off there tomorrow in fulfilment of his wish; but I esteemed it a duty to visit you first.'

'I am very, very much obliged to you, my dear. Relations ought never to forget one another. And do you know I am surprised how well you speak Russian. *C'est étonnant.*'

Varvara Pavlovna sighed.

'I have been too long abroad, Marya Dmitrievna, I know that; but my heart has always been Russian, and I have not forgotten my country.'

'Ah, ah; that is good. Fedor Ivanitch did not, however, expect you at all. Yes; you may trust my experience, *la patrie avant tout.* Ah, show me, if you please—what a charming mantle you have.'

'Dou you like it?' Varvara Pavlovna slipped it quickly off her shoulders; 'it is a very simple little thing from Madame Baudran.'

'One can see it at once. From Madame Baudran? How sweet, and what a taste! I am sure you have brought a number of fascinating things with you. If I could only see them.'

'All my things are at your service, dearest auntie. If you permit, I can show some patterns to your maid. I have a woman with me from Paris—a wonderfully clever dress-maker.'

'You are very good, my dear. But, really, I am ashamed.' . . .

'Ashamed!' repeated Varvara Pavlovna reproachfully. 'If you want to make me happy, dispose of me as if I were your property.'

Marya Dmitrievna was completely melted.

'*Vous êtes charmante,*' she said. 'But why don't you take off your hat and gloves?'

'What? you will allow me?' asked Varvara Pavlovna, and slightly, as though with emotion, clasped her hands.

'Of course, you will dine with us, I hope. I—I will introduce you to my daughter.' Marya Dmitrievna was a little confused. 'Well! we are in for it! here goes!' she thought. 'She is not very well today.'

'*O ma tante*, how good you are!' cried Varvara Pavlovna, and she raised her handkerchief to her eyes.

A page announced the arrival of Gedeonovsky. The old gossip came in bowing and smiling. Marya Dmitrievna presented him to her visitor. He was thrown into confusion for the first moment; but Varvara Pavlovna behaved with such coquettish respectfulness to him, that his ears began to tingle, and gossip, slander, and civility dropped like honey from his lips. Varvara Pavlovna listened to him with a restrained smile and began by degrees to talk herself. She spoke modestly of Paris, of her travels, of Baden; twice she made Marya Dmitrievna laugh, and each time she sighed a little afterwards, and seemed to be inwardly reproaching herself for misplaced levity. She obtained permission to bring Ada; taking off her gloves, with her smooth hands, redolent of soap *à la guimauve*, she showed how and where flounces were worn and ruches and lace and rosettes. She promised to bring a bottle of the new English scent, Victoria Essence; and was as happy as a child when Marya Dmitrievna consented to accept it as a gift. She was moved to tears over the recollection of the emotion she experienced, when, for the first time, she heard the Russian bells. 'They went so deeply to my heart,' she explained.

At that instant Lisa came in.

Ever since the morning, from the very instant when, chill with horror, she had read Lavretsky's note, Lisa had been preparing herself for the meeting with his wife. She had a presentiment that she would see her. She resolved not to avoid her, as a punishment of her, as she called them, sinful hopes. The sudden crisis in her destiny had shaken her to the foundations. In some two hours her face seemed to have grown thin. But she did not shed a single tear. 'It's what I deserve!' she said to herself, repressing with difficulty and dismay some bitter impulses of hatred which frightened her in her soul. 'Well, I must go down!' she thought directly she heard of Madame Lavretsky's arrival, and she went down. . . . She stood a long while at the drawing-room door before she could summon up courage to open it. With the thought, 'I have done her wrong', she crossed the threshold and forced herself to look at her, forced herself to smile. Varvara Pavlovna went to meet her directly she caught sight of her, and bowed to her slightly, but still respectfully. 'Allow me to introduce myself,' she began in an insinuating voice, 'your *maman* is so indulgent to me that I hope that you too will be . . . good to me.' The expression of Varvara Pavlovna, when she uttered these last words, cold and at the same time soft, her hypocritical smile, the action of her hands, and her shoulders, her very dress, her whole being aroused such a feeling of repulsion in Lisa that she could make no reply to her, and only held out her hand with an effort. 'This young lady disdains me,' thought Varvara Pavlovna, warmly pressing Lisa's cold fingers, and turning to Marya Dmitrievna, she observed in an undertone, *'mais elle est délicieuse!'* Lisa faintly flushed; she heard ridicule, insult in this exclamation. But she resolved not to trust her impressions, and sat down by the window at her embroidery-frame. Even here Varvara Pavlovna did not leave her in peace. She began to admire her taste, her skill. . . . Lisa's heart beat violently and painfully. She could scarcely control herself, she could scarcely sit in her place. It seemed to her that Varvara Pavlovna knew all, and was mocking at her in secret triumph. To her relief, Gedeonovsky began to talk to Varvara Pavlovna, and drew off her attention. Lisa bent over her frame, and secretly watched her. 'That woman,' she thought, 'was loved by *him*.' But she at once drove away the very thought of Lavretsky; she was afraid of losing her control over herself, she felt that her head was going round. Marya Dmitrievna began to talk of music.

'I have heard, my dear,' she began, 'that you are a wonderful performer.'

'It is long since I have played,' replied Varvara Pavlovna, seating herself without delay at the piano, and running her fingers smartly over the keys. 'Do you wish it?'

'If you will be so kind.'

Varvara Pavlovna played a brilliant and difficult *étude* by Hertz very correctly. She had great power and execution.

'*Sylphide!*' cried Gedeonovsky.

'Marvellous!' Marya Dmitrievna chimed in. 'Well, Varvara Pavlovna I confess,' she observed, for the first time calling her by her name, 'you have astonished me; you might give concerts. We have a musician here, an old German, a queer fellow, but a very clever musician. He gives Lisa lessons. He will be simply crazy over you.'

'Lisaveta Mihalovna is also musical?' asked Varvara Pavlovna, turning her head slightly towards her.

'Yes, she plays fairly, and is fond of music; but what is that beside you? But there is one young man here too—with whom we must make you acquainted. He is an artist in soul, and composes very charmingly. He alone will be able to appreciate you fully.'

'A young man?' said Varvara Pavlovna: 'Who is he? Some poor man?'

'Oh dear no, our chief beau, and not only among us—*et à Petersbourg*. A *Kammerjunker*, and received in the best society. You must have heard of him: Panshin, Vladimir Nikolaitch. He is here on a government commission . . . a future minister, I daresay!'

'And an artist?'

'An artist at heart, and so well-bred. You shall see him. He has been here very often of late: I invited him for this evening; I *hope* he will come,' added Marya Dmitrievna with a gentle sigh, and an oblique smile of bitterness.

Lisa knew the meaning of this smile, but it was nothing to her now.

'And young?' repeated Varvara Pavlovna, lightly modulating from tone to tone.

'Twenty-eight, and of the most prepossessing appearance. *Un jeune homme accompli*, indeed.'

'An exemplary young man, one may say,' observed Gedeonovsky.

Varvara Pavlovna began suddenly playing a noisy waltz of Strauss, opening with such a loud and rapid trill that Gedeonovsky was quite startled. In the very middle of the waltz she suddenly passed into a pathetic motive, and finished up with an air from 'Lucia' *Fra poco.* . . . . She reflected that lively music was not in keeping with her position. The air from 'Lucia', with emphasis on the sentimental passages, moved Marya Dmitrievna greatly.

'What soul!' she observed in an undertone to Gedeonovsky.

'A *sylphide!*' repeated Gedeonovsky, raising his eyes towards heaven.

The dinner hour arrived. Marfa Timofyevna came down from upstairs, when the soup was already on the table. She treated Varvara Pavlovna very drily, replied in half-sentences to her civilities, and did not look at her. Varvara Pavlovna soon realised that there was nothing to be got out of this old lady, and gave up trying to talk to her. To make up for this Marya Dmitrievna became still more cordial to her guest; her aunt's discourtesy irritated her. Marfa Timofyevna, however, did not only avoid looking at Varvara Pavlovna; she did not look at Lisa either, though her eyes seemed literally blazing. She sat as though she were of stone, yellow and pale, her lips compressed, and ate nothing. Lisa seemed calm; and in reality, her heart was more at rest; a strange apathy, the apathy of the condemned had come upon her. At dinner Varvara Pavlovna spoke little; she seemed to have grown timid again, and her countenance was overspread with an expression of modest melancholy. Gedeonovsky alone enlivened the conversation with his tales, though he constantly looked timorously towards Marfa Timofyevna and coughed—he was always overtaken by a fit of coughing when he was going to tell a lie in her presence—but she did not hinder him by any interruption. After dinner it seemed that Varvara Pavlovna was quite devoted to preference; at this Mary Dmitrievna was so delighted that she felt quite overcome, and thought to herself, 'Really what a fool Fedor Ivanitch must be; not able to appreciate a woman like this!'

She sat down to play cards together with her and Gedeonovsky, and Marfa Timofyevna led Lisa away upstairs with her, saying that she looked shocking, and that she must certainly have a headache.

'Yes, she has an awful headache,' observed Marya Dmitrievna, turning to Varvara Pavlovna and rolling her eyes, 'I myself have often just such sick headaches.'

'Really!' rejoined Varvara Pavlovna.

Lisa went into her aunt's room, and sank powerless into a chair. Marfa Timofyevna gazed long at her in silence, slowly she knelt down before her—and began still in the same silence to kiss her hands alternately. Lisa bent forward, crimsoning —and began to weep, but she did not make Marfa Timofyevna get up, she did not take away her hands; she felt that she had not the right to take them away, that she had not the right to hinder the old lady from expressing her penitence, and her sympathy, from begging forgiveness for what had passed the day before. And Marfa Timofyevna could not kiss enough those poor, pale, powerless hands, and silent tears flowed from her eyes and from Lisa's; while the cat Matross purred in the wide arm-chair among the knitting wool, and the long flame of the little lamp faintly stirred and flickered before the holy picture. In the next room, behind the door, stood Nastasya Karpovna, and she too was furtively wiping her eyes with her check pocket-handkerchief rolled up in a ball.

<h1 style="text-align:center">* 40 *</h1>

Meanwhile, downstairs, preference was going on merrily in the drawing-room; Marya Dmitrievna was winning, and was in high good-humour. A servant came in and announced that Panshin was below.

Marya Dmitrievna dropped her cards and moved restlessly in her arm-chair; Varvara Pavlovna looked at her with a half-smile, then turned her eyes towards the door. Panshin made his appearance in a black frock-coat buttoned up to the throat, and a high English collar. 'It was hard for me to obey; but you see I have come,' this was what was expressed by his unsmiling, freshly-shaven countenance.

'Well, *Woldemar*,' cried Marya Dmitrievna, 'you used to come in unannounced!'

Panshin only replied to Marya Dmitrievna by a single glance. He bowed courteously to her, but did not kiss her hand. She presented him to Varvara Pavlovna; he stepped back a pace, bowed to her with the same courtesy, but with still greater elegance and respect, and took a seat near the card-table. The game of preference was soon over. Panshin inquired after Lisaveta Mihalovna, learnt that she was not quite well, and expressed his regret. Then he began to talk to Varvara Pavlovna, diplomatically weighing each word and giving it its full value, and politely hearing her answers to the end. But the dignity of his diplomatic tone did not impress Varvara Pavlovna, and she did not adopt it. On the contrary, she looked him in the face with light-hearted attention and talked easily, while her delicate nostrils were quivering as though with suppressed laughter. Marya Dmitrievna began to enlarge on her talent; Panshin courteously inclined his head, so far as his collar would permit him, declared that, 'he felt sure of it beforehand', and almost turned the conversation to the diplomatic topic of Metternich himself. Varvara Pavlovna, with an expressive look in her velvety eyes, said in a low voice, 'Why, but you too are an artist, *un confrère,*' adding still lower, '*venez!*' with a nod towards the piano. The single word *venez* thrown at him, instantly, as though by magic, effected a complete transformation in Panshin's whole appearance. His care-worn air disappeared; he smiled and grew lively, unbuttoned his coat, and repeating 'a poor artist, alas! Now you, I have heard, are a real artist;' he followed Varvara Pavlovna to the piano. . . .

'Make him sing his song, "How the Moon Floats", ' cried Marya Dmitrievna.

'Do you sing?' said Varvara Pavlovna, enfolding him in a rapid radiant look. 'Sit down.'

Panshin began to cry off.

'Sit down,' she repeated insistently, tapping on a chair behind him.

He sat down, coughed, tugged at his collar, and sang his song.

'*Charmant,*' pronounced Varvara Pavlovna, 'you sing very well, *vous avez du style,* again.'

She walked round the piano and stood just opposite Panshin. He sang it again, increasing the melodramatic tremor in his voice. Varvara Pavlovna stared steadily at him, leaning her elbows on the piano and holding her white hands on a level with her lips. Panshin finished the song.

'*Charmant, charmante idée,*' she said with the calm self-confidence of a connoisseur. 'Tell me, have you composed anything for a woman's voice, for a mezzo-soprano?'

'I hardly compose at all,' replied Panshin. 'That was only thrown off in the intervals of business . . . but do you sing?'

'Yes.'

'Oh! sing us something,' urged Marya Dmitrievna.

Varvara Pavlovna pushed her hair back off her glowing cheeks and gave her head a little shake.

'Our voices ought to go well together,' she observed, turning to Panshin; 'let us sing a duet. Do you know *Son geloso*, or *La ci darem*, or *Mira la bianca luna?*'

'I used to sing *Mira la bianca luna*, once,' replied Panshin, 'but long ago; I have forgotten it.'

'Never mind, we will rehearse it in a low voice. Allow me.'

Varvara Pavlovna sat down at the piano, Panshin stood by her. They sang through the duet in an undertone, and Varvara Pavlovna corrected him several times as they did so, then they sang it aloud, and then twice repeated the performance of *Mira la bianca lu-u-una*. Varvara Pavlovna's voice had lost its freshness, but she managed it with great skill. Panshin at first was hesitating, and a little out of tune, then he warmed up, and if his singing was not quite beyond criticism, at least he shrugged his shoulders, swayed his whole person, and lifted his hand from time to time in the most genuine style. Varvara Pavlovna played two or three little things of Thalberg's, and coquettishly rendered a little ballad. Marya Dmitrievna did not know how to express her delight; she several times tried to send for Lisa. Gedeonovsky, too, was at a loss for words, and could only nod his head, but all at once he gave an unexpected yawn, and hardly had time to cover his mouth with his hand. This yawn did not escape Varvara Pavlovna; she at once turned her back on the piano, observing, '*Assez de musique comme ça*; let us talk', and she folded her arms. '*Oui, assez de musique*,' repeated Panshin gaily, and at once he dropped into a chat, alert, light, and in French. 'Precisely as in the best Parisian salon,' thought Marya Dmitrievna, as she listened to their fluent and quick-witted sentences. Panshin had a sense of complete satisfaction; his eyes shone, and he smiled. At first he passed his hand across his face, contracted his brows, and sighed spasmodically whenever he chanced to encounter Marya Dmitrievna's eyes. But later on he forgot her altogether, and gave himself up entirely to the enjoyment of a half-worldly, half-artistic chat. Varvara Pavlovna proved to be a great philosopher; she had a ready answer for everything; she never hesitated, never doubted about any thing; one could see that she had conversed much with clever men of all kinds. All her ideas, all her feelings revolved round Paris. Panshin turned the conversation upon literature; it seemed that, like himself, she read only French books. George Sand drove her to exasperation, Balzac she respected, but he wearied her; in Sue and Scribe she saw great knowledge of human nature, Dumas and Féval she adored. In her heart she preferred Paul de Kock to all of them, but of course she did not even mention his name. To tell the truth, literature had no great interest for her. Varvara Pavlovna very skilfully avoided all that could even remotely recall her position; there was no reference to love in her remarks; on the contrary, they were rather expressive of austerity in regard to the allurements of passion, of disillusionment and resignation. Panshin disputed with her; she did not agree with him . . . but, strange to say! . . . at the very time when words of censure—often of severe censure—were coming from her lips, these words had a soft caressing sound, and her eyes spoke . . . precisely what those lovely eyes spoke, it was hard to say; but at least their utterances were anything but severe, and were full of undefined sweetness.

Panshin tried to interpret their secret meaning, he tried to make his own eyes speak, but he felt he was not successful; he was conscious that Varvara Pavlovna, in the character of a real lioness from abroad, stood high above him, and consequently was not completely master of himself. Varvara Pavlovna had a habit in conversation of lightly touching the sleeve of the person she was talking to; these momentary contacts had a most disquieting influence on Vladimir Nikolaitch. Varvara Pavlovna possessed the faculty of getting on easily with everyone; before two hours had passed it seemed to Panshin that he had known her for an age, and Lisa, the same Lisa whom, at anyrate, he had loved, to whom he had the evening before offered his hand, had vanished as it were into a mist. Tea was brought in; the conversation became still more unconstrained. Marya Dmitrievna rang for the page and gave orders to ask Lisa to come down if her head were better. Panshin, hearing Lisa's name, fell to discussing self-sacrifice and the question which was more capable of sacrifice—man or woman. Marya Dmitrievna at once became excited, began to maintain that woman is the more ready for sacrifice, declared that she would prove it in a couple of words, got confused and finished up by a rather unfortunate comparison. Varvara Pavlovna took up a music-book and half-hiding behind it and bending towards Panshin, she observed in a whisper, as she nibbled a biscuit, with a serene smile on her lips and in her eyes, '*Elle n'a pas inventé la poudre, la bonne dame.*' Panshin was a little taken aback and amazed at Varvara Pavlovna's audacity; but he did not realise how much contempt for himself was concealed in this unexpected outbreak, and forgetting Marya Dmitrievna's kindness and devotion, forgetting all the dinners she had given him, and the money she had lent him, he replied (luckless mortal!) with the same smile and in the same tone, '*Je crois bien,*' and not even, *je crois bien*, but *j'crois ben*!

Varvara Pavlovna flung him a friendly glance and got up. Lisa came in: Marfa Timofyevna had tried in vain to hinder her; she was resolved to go through with her sufferings to the end. Varvara Pavlovna went to meet her together with Panshin, on whose face the former diplomatic expression had reappeared.

'How are you?' he asked Lisa.

'I am better now, thank you,' she replied.

'We have been having a little music here; it's a pity you did not hear Varvara Pavlovna, she sings superbly, *en artiste consommée.*'

'Come here, my dear,' sounded Marya Dmitrievna's voice.

Varvara Pavlovna went to her at once with the submissiveness of a child, and sat down on a little stool at her feet. Marya Dmitrievna had called her so as to leave her daughter, at least for a moment, alone with Panshin; she was still secretly hoping that she would come round. Besides, an idea had entered her head, to which she was anxious to give expression at once.

'Do you know,' she whispered to Varvara Pavlovna, 'I want to endeavour to reconcile you and your husband; I won't answer for my success, but I will make an effort. He has, you know, a great respect for me.'

Varvara Pavlovna slowly raised her eyes to Marya Dmitrievna, and eloquently clasped her hands.

'You would be my saviour, *ma tante*,' she said in a mournful voice: 'I don't know how to thank you for all your kindness; but I have been too guilty towards Fedor Ivanitch; he cannot forgive me.'

'But did you—in reality——' Marya Dmitrievna was beginning inquisitively.

'Don't question me,' Varvara Pavlovna interrupted her, and she cast down her eyes. 'I was young, frivolous. But I don't want to justify myself.'

'Well, anyway, why not try? Don't despair,' rejoined Marya Dmitrievna, and she was on the point of patting her on the cheek, but after a glance at her she had not the courage. 'She is humble, very humble,' she thought, 'but still she is a lioness.'

'Are you ill?' Panshin was saying to Lisa meanwhile.

'Yes, I am not well.'

'I understand you,' he brought out after a rather protracted silence. 'Yes, I understand you.'

'What?'

'I understand you,' Panshin repeated significantly; he simply did not know what to say.

Lisa felt embarrassed, and then 'so be it!' she thought. Panshin assumed a mysterious air and kept silent, looking severely away.

'I fancy though it's struck eleven,' remarked Marya Dmitrievna.

Her guests took the hint and began to say goodbye. Varvara Pavlovna had to promise that she would come to dinner the following day and bring Ada. Gedeonovsky, who had all but fallen asleep sitting in his corner, offered to escort her home. Panshin took leave solemnly of all, but at the steps as he put Varvara Pavlovna into her carriage he pressed her hand, and cried after her, '*au revoir*!' Gedeonovsky sat beside her all the way home. She amused herself by pressing the tip of her little foot as though accidentally on his foot; he was thrown into confusion and began paying her compliments. She tittered and made eyes at him when the light of a street lamp fell into the carriage. The waltz she had played was ringing in her head, and exciting her; whatever position she might find herself in, she had only to imagine lights, a ballroom, rapid whirling to the strains of music—and her blood was on fire, her eyes glittered strangely, a smile strayed about her lips, and something of bacchanalian grace was visible over her whole frame. When she reached home Varvara Pavlovna bounded lightly out of the carriage—only real lionesses know how to bound like that—and turning round to Gedeonovsky she burst suddenly into a ringing laugh right in his face.

'An attractive person,' thought the counsellor of state as he made his way to his lodgings, where his servant was awaiting him with a glass of opodeldoc: 'It's well I'm a steady fellow —only, what was she laughing at?'

Marfa Timofyevna spent the whole night sitting beside Lisa's bed.

* *41* *

Lavretsky spent a day and a half at Vassilyevskoe, and employed almost all the time in wandering about the neighbourhood. He could not stop long in one place: he was devoured by anguish; he was torn unceasingly by impotent violent impulses. He remembered the feeling which had taken possession of him the day after his arrival in the country; he remembered his plans then and was intensely exasperated with himself. What had been able to tear him away from what he recognized as his duty—as the one task set before him in the future? The thirst for happiness—again the same thirst for happiness.

'It seems Mihalevitch was right,' he thought; 'you wanted

a second time to taste happiness in life,' he said to himself, 'you forgot that it is a luxury, an undeserved bliss, if it even comes once to a man. It was not complete, it was not genuine, you say; but prove your right to full genuine happiness! Look round and see who is happy, who enjoys life about you? Look at that peasant going to the mowing; is he contented with his fate? . . . What! would you care to change places with him? Remember your mother; how infinitely little she asked of life, and what a life fell to her lot. You were only bragging it seems when you said to Panshin that you had come back to Russia to cultivate the soil; you have come back to dangle after young girls in your old age. Directly the news of your freedom came, you threw up everything, forgot everything; you ran like a boy after a butterfly.' . . .

The image of Lisa continually presented itself in the midst of his broodings. He drove it away with an effort together with another importunate figure, other serenely wily, beautiful, hated features. Old Anton noticed that the master was not himself: after sighing several times outside the door and several times in the doorway, he made up his mind to go up to him, and advised him to take a hot drink of something. Lavretsky swore at him; ordered him out; afterwards he begged his pardon, but that only made Anton still more sorrowful. Lavretsky could not stay in the drawing-room; it seemed to him that his great-grandfather Andrey, was looking contemptuously from the canvas at his feeble descendant. 'Bah: you swim in shallow water,' the distorted lips seemed to be saying. 'Is it possible,' he thought, 'that I cannot master myself, that I am going to give in to this . . . nonsense?' (Those who are badly wounded in war always call their wounds 'nonsense'. If man did not deceive himself, he could not live on earth.) 'Am I really a boy? Ah, well; I saw quite close, I almost held in my hands the possibility of happiness for my whole life; yes, in the lottery too—turn the wheel a little and the beggar perhaps would be a rich man. If it does not happen, then it does not—and it's all over. I will set to work, with my teeth clenched, and make myself be quiet; it's as well, it's not the first time I have had to hold myself in. And why have I run away, why am I stopping here sticking my head in a bush, like an ostrich? A fearful thing to face trouble . . . nonsense! Anton,' he called aloud, 'order the coach to be brought round at once. Yes,' he thought again, 'I must grin and bear it, I must keep myself well in hand.'

With such reasonings Lavretsky tried to ease his pain; but it was deep and intense; and even Apraxya who had out-lived all emotion as well as intelligence shook her head and followed him mournfully with her eyes, as he took his seat in the coach to drive to the town. The horses galloped away; he sat upright and motionless, and looked fixedly at the road before him.

* 42 *

Lisa had written to Lavretsky the day before, to tell him to come in the evening; but he first went home to his lodgings. He found neither his wife nor his daughter at home; from the servants he learned that she had gone with the child to the Kalitins'. This information astounded and maddened him. 'Varvara Pavlovna has made up her mind not to let me live at all, it seems,' he thought with a passion of hatred in his heart. He began to walk up and down, and his hands and feet were constantly knocking up against child's toys, books and feminine belongings; he called Justine and told her to clear away all this 'litter'. 'Oui, monsieur,' she said with a grimace, and began to set the room in order, stooping gracefully, and letting Lavretsky feel in every movement that she regarded him as an unpolished bear. He looked with aversion at her faded, but still 'piquante', ironical, Parisian face, at her white elbow-sleeves, her silk apron, and little light cap. He sent her away at last, and after long hesitation (as Varvara Pavlovna still did not return) he decided to go to the Kalitins'—not to see Marya Dmitrievna (he would not for anything in the world have gone into that drawing-room, the room where his wife was), but to go up to Marfa Timo-fyevna's. He remembered that the back staircase from the servants' entrance led straight to her apartment. He acted on this plan; fortune favoured him; he met Shurotchka in the courtyard; she conducted him up to Marfa Timofyevna's. He found her, contrary to her usual habit, alone; she was sitting without a cap in a corner, bent, and her arms crossed over her breast. The old lady was much upset on seeing Lavretsky, she got up quickly and began to move to and fro in the room as if she were looking for her cap.

'Ah, it's you,' she began, fidgeting about and avoiding meeting his eyes, 'well, how do you do? Well, well, what's to be done! Where were you yesterday? Well, she has come, so there, there! Well, it must . . . one way or another.'

Lavretsky dropped into a chair.

'Well, sit down, sit down,' the old lady went on. 'Did you come straight upstairs? Well, there, of course. So . . . you came to see me? Thanks.'

The old lady was silent for a little; Lavretsky did not know what to say to her; but she understood him.

'Lisa . . . yes, Lisa was here just now,' pursued Marfa Timofyevna, tying and untying the tassels of her reticule. 'She was not quite well. Shurotchka, where are you? Come here, my girl; why can't you sit still a little? My head aches too. It must be the effect of the singing and music.'

'What singing, auntie?'

'Why, we have been having those—upon my word, what do you call them—duets here. And all in Italian: chi-chi—and cha-cha—like magpies for all the world with their long drawn-out notes as if they'd pull your very soul out. That's Panshin, and your wife too. And how quickly everything was settled; just as though it were all among relations, without ceremony. However, one may well say, even a dog will try to find a home; and won't be lost so long as folks don't drive it out.'

'Still, I confess I did not expect this,' rejoined Lavretsky; 'there must be great effrontery to do this.'

'No, my darling, it's not effrontery, it's calculation, God forgive her! They say you are sending her off to Lavriky; is it true?'

'Yes, I am giving up that property to Varvara Pavlovna.'

'Has she asked you for money?'

'Not yet.'

'Well, that won't be long in coming. But I have only now got a look at you. Are you quite well?'

'Yes.'

'Shurotchka!' cried Marfa Timofyevna suddenly, 'run and tell Lisaveta Mihalovna—at least, no, ask her . . . is she downstairs?'

'Yes.'

'Well, then; ask her where she put my book? she will know.'

'Very well.'

The old lady grew fidgety again and began opening a drawer in the chest. Lavretsky sat still without stirring in his place.

All at once light footsteps were heard on the stairs—and Lisa came in.

Lavretsky stood up and bowed; Lisa remained at the door.

'Lisa, Lisa, darling,' began Marfa Timofyevna eagerly, 'where is my book? where did you put by book?'

'What book, auntie?'

'Why, goodness me, thàt book! But I didn't call you though . . . There, it doesn't matter. What are you doing downstairs? Here Fedor Ivanitch has come. How is your head?'

'It's nothing.'

'You keep saying it's nothing. What have you going on downstairs—music?'

'No—they are playing cards.'

'Well, she's ready for anything. Shurotchka, I see you want a run in the garden—run along.'

'Oh, no, Marfa Timofyevna.'

'Don't argue, if you please, run along. Nastasya Karpovna has gone out into the garden all by herself; you keep her company. You must treat the old with respect.'—Shurotchka departed—'But where is my cap? Where has it got to?'

'Let me look for it,' said Lisa.

'Sit down, sit down; I have still the use of my legs. It must be inside in my bedroom.'

And flinging a sidelong glance in Lavretsky's direction, Marfa Timofyevna went out. She left the door open; but suddenly she came back to it and shut it.

Lisa leant back against her chair and quietly covered her face with her hands; Lavretsky remained where he was.

'This is how we were to meet again!' he brought out at last.

Lisa took her hands from her face.

'Yes,' she said faintly: 'we were quickly punished'.

'Punished,' said Lavretsky. . . . 'What had you done to be punished'?

Lisa raised her eyes to him. There was neither sorrow nor disquiet expressed in them: they seemed smaller and dimmer. Her face was pale; and pale too her slightly parted lips.

Lavretsky's heart shuddered for pity and love.

'You wrote to me; all is over,' he whispered, 'yes, all is over—before it had begun.'

'We must forget all that,' Lisa brought out; 'I am glad that you have come; I wanted to write to you, but it is better so. Only we must take advantage quickly of these minutes. It is left for both of us to do our duty. You, Fedor Ivanitch, must be reconciled with your wife.'

'Lisa!'

'I beg you to do so; by that alone can we expiate . . . all that has happened. You will think about it—and will not refuse me.'

'Lisa, for God's sake—you are asking what is impossible. I am ready to do everything you tell me; but to be reconciled to her *now*! . . . I consent to everything, I have forgotten everything; but I cannot force my heart. . . . Indeed, this is cruel!'

'I do not even ask of you, . . . what you say; do not live with her, if you cannot; but be reconciled,' replied Lisa, and again she hid her eyes in her hand.—'Remember your little girl; do it for my sake.'

'Very well,' Lavretsky muttered between his teeth: 'I will do that, I suppose in that I shall fulfil my duty. But you— what does your duty consist in?'

'That I know myself.'

Lavretsky started suddenly.

'You cannot be making up your mind to marry Panshin?' he said.

Lisa gave an almost imperceptible smile.

'Oh, no!' she said.

'Ah, Lisa, Lisa!' cried Lavretsky, 'how happy you might have been!'

Lisa looked at him again.

'Now you see yourself, Fedor Ivanitch, that happiness does not depend on us, but on God.'

'Yes, because you——'

The door from the adjoining room opened quickly and Marfa Timofyevna came in with her cap in her hand.

'I have found it at last,' she said, standing between Lavretsky and Lisa; 'I had laid it down myself. That's what age does for one, alack!—though youth's not much better.'

'Well, and are you going to Lavriky yourself with your wife?' she added, turning to Lavretsky.

'To Lavriky with her? I don't know,' he said, after a moment's hesitation.

'You are not going downstairs?'

'Today—no, I'm not.'

'Well, well, you know best; but you, Lisa, I think, ought to go down. Ah, merciful powers, I have forgotten to feed my bullfinch. There, stop a minute, I'll soon——' And Marfa Timofyevna ran off without putting on her cap.

Lavretsky walked quickly up to Lisa.

'Lisa,' he began in a voice of entreaty, 'we are parting for ever, my heart is torn—give me your hand at parting.'

Lisa raised her head, her wearied eyes, their light almost extinct, rested upon him. . . . 'No,' she uttered, and she drew back the hand she was holding out. 'No, Lavretsky (it was the first time she had used this name), I will not give you my hand. What is the good? Go away, I beseech you. You know I love you . . . yes, I love you,' she added with an effort; 'but no . . . no.'

She pressed her handkerchief to her lips.

'Give me, at least, that handkerchief.'

The door creaked . . . the handkerchief slid on to Lisa's lap. Lavretsky snatched it before it had time to fall to the floor, thrust it quickly into a side pocket, and turning round met Marfa Timofyevna's eyes.

'Lisa, darling, I fancy your mother is calling you,' the old lady declared.

Lisa at once got up and went away.

Marfa Timofyevna sat down again in her corner. Lavretsky began to take leave of her.

'Fedor,' she said suddenly.

'What is it?'

'Are you an honest man?'

'What?'

'I ask you, are you an honest man?'

'I hope so.'

'H'm. But give me your word of honour that you will be an honest man.'

'Certainly. But why?'

'I know why. And you too, my dear friend, if you think well, you're no fool—will understand why I ask it of you. And now, goodbye, my dear. Thanks for your visit; and remember you have given your word, Fedya, and kiss me. Oh, my dear, it's hard for you, I know; but there, it's not easy for any one. Once I used to envy the flies; I thought, it's for them it's good to be alive, but one night I heard a fly complaining in a spider's web—no, I think, they too have their troubles. There's no help, Fedya; but remember your promise all the same. Goodbye.'

Lavretsky went down the back staircase, and had reached the gates when a man-servant overtook him.

'Marya Dmitrievna told me to ask you to go in to her,' he commenced to Lavretsky.

'Tell her, my boy, that just now I can't——' Fedor Ivanitch was beginning.

'Her excellency told me to ask you very particularly,' continued the servant. 'She gave orders to say she was at home.'

'Have the visitors gone?' asked Lavretsky.

'Certainly, sir,' replied the servant with a grin.

Lavretsky shrugged his shoulders and followed him.

✱ *43* ✱

Marya Dmitrievna was sitting alone in her boudoir in an easy-chair, sniffing *eau de cologne*; a glass of orange-flower-water was standing on a little table near her. She was agitated and seemed nervous.

Lavretsky came in.

'You wanted to see me,' he said, bowing coldly.

'Yes,' replied Marya Dmitrievna, and she sipped a little water: 'I heard that you had gone straight up to my aunt; I gave orders that you should be asked to come in; I wanted to have a little talk with you. Sit down, please,' Marya Dmitrievna took breath. 'You know,' she went on, 'your wife has come.'

'I was aware of that,' remarked Lavretsky.

'Well, then, that is, I wanted to say, she came to me, and I received her; that is what I wanted to explain to you, Fedor Ivanitch. Thank God I have, I may say, gained universal respect, and for no consideration in the world would I do anything improper. Though I foresaw that it would be disagreeable to you, still I could not make up my mind to deny myself to her, Fedor Ivanitch; she is a relation of mine—through you; put yourself in my position, what right had I to shut my doors on her—you will agree with me?'

'You are exciting yourself needlessly, Marya Dmitrievna,' replied Lavretsky; 'you acted very well, I am not angry. I have not the least intention of depriving Varvara Pavlovna of the opportunity of seeing her friends; I did not come in to you today simply because I did not care to meet her—that was all.'

'Ah, how glad I am to hear you say that, Fedor Ivanitch,' cried Marya Dmitrievna, 'but I always expected it of your noble sentiments. And as for my being excited—that's not to be wondered at; I am a woman and a mother. And your wife . . . of course I cannot judge between you and her—as I said to her herself; but she is such a delightful woman that she can produce nothing but a pleasant impression.'

Lavretsky gave a laugh and played with his hat.

'And this is what I wanted to say to you besides, Fedor Ivanitch,' continued Marya Dmitrievna, moving slightly nearer up to him, 'if you had seen the modesty of her behaviour, how respectful she is! Really, it is quite touching. And if you had heard how she spoke of you! I have been to blame towards him, she said, altogether; I did not know how

[147]

to appreciate him, she said; he is an angel, she said, and not a man. Really, that is what she said—an angel. Her penitence is such . . . Ah, upon my word, I have never seen such penitence!'

'Well, Marya Dmitrievna,' observed Lavretsky, 'if I may be inquisitive: I am told that Varvara Pavlovna has been singing in your drawing-room; did she sing during the time of her penitence, or how was it?'

'Ah, I wonder you are not ashamed to talk like that! She sang and played the piano only to do me a kindness, because I positively entreated, almost commanded her to do so. I saw that she was sad, so sad; I thought how to distract her mind —and I had heard that she had such marvellous talent! I assure you, Fedor Ivanitch, she is utterly crushed, ask Sergei Petrovitch even; a heart-broken woman, *tout à fait*: what do you say?'

Lavretsky only shrugged his shoulders.

'And then what a little angel is that Adotchka of yours, what a darling! How sweet she is, what a clever little thing; how she speaks French; and understands Russian too—she called me "auntie" in Russian. And you know that as for shyness—almost all children at her age are shy—there's not a trace of it. She's so like you, Fedor Ivanitch, it's amazing. The eyes, the forehead—well, it's you over again, precisely you. I am not particularly fond of little children, I must own; but I simply lost my heart to your little girl.'

'Marya Dmitrievna,' Lavretsky blurted out suddenly, 'allow me to ask you what is your object in talking to me like this?'

'What object?' Marya Dmitrievna sniffed her *eau de cologne* again, and took a sip of water. 'Why, I am speaking to you, Fedor Ivanitch, because—I am a relation of yours, you know, I take the warmest interest in you—I know your heart is of the best. Listen to me, *mon cousin*. I am at any rate a woman of experience, and I shall not talk at random: forgive her, forgive your wife.' Marya Dmitrievna's eyes suddenly filled with tears. 'Only think: her youth, her inexperience . . . and who knows, perhaps, bad example; she had not a mother who could bring her up in the right way. Forgive her, Fedor Ivanitch, she has been punished enough.'

The tears were trickling down Marya Dmitrievna's cheeks: she did not wipe them away; she was fond of weeping. Lavretsky sat as if on thorns. 'Good God,' he thought, 'what torture, what a day I have had today!'

'You make no reply,' Marya Dmitrievna began again. 'How am I to understand you? Can you really be so cruel? No, I will not believe it. I feel that my words have influenced you, Fedor Ivanitch. God reward you for your goodness, and now receive your wife from my hands.'

Involuntarily Lavretsky jumped up from his chair; Marya Dmitrievna also rose and running quickly behind a screen, she led forth Varvara Pavlovna. Pale, almost lifeless, with downcast eyes, she seemed to have renounced all thought, all will of her own, and to have surrendered herself completely to Marya Dmitrievna.

Lavretsky stepped back a pace.

'You have been here all the time!' he cried.

'Do not blame her,' explained Marya Dmitrievna; 'she was most unwilling to stay, but I forced her to remain. I put her behind the screen. She assured me that this would only anger you more; I would not even listen to her; I know you better than she does. Take your wife back from my hands; come, Varya, do not fear, fall at your husband's feet (she gave a pull at her arm) and my blessing' . . .

'Stop a minute, Marya Dmitrievna,' said Lavretsky in a low but startlingly impressive voice. 'I dare say you are fond of affecting scenes' (Lavretsky was right, Marya Dmitrievna still retained her schoolgirl's passion for a little melodramatic effect), 'they amuse you; but they may be anything but pleasant for other people. But I am not going to talk to you; in *this* scene you are not the principal character. What do you want to get out of me, madam?' he added, turning to his wife. 'Haven't I done all I could for you? Don't tell me you did not contrive this interview; I shall not believe you—and you know that I cannot possibly believe you. What is it you want? You are clever—you do nothing without an object. You must realise, that as for living with you, as I once lived with you, that I cannot do; not because I am angry with you, but because I have become a different man. I told you so the day after your return, and you yourself, at that moment, agreed with me in your heart. But you want to reinstate yourself in public opinion; it is not enough for you to live in my house, you want to live with me under the same roof—isn't that it?'

'I want your forgiveness,' pronounced Varvara Pavlovna, not raising her eyes.

'She wants your forgiveness,' repeated Marya Dmitrievna.

'And not for my own sake, but for Ada's,' murmured Varvara Pavlovna.

'And not for her own sake, but for your Ada's,' repeated Marya Dmitrievna.

'Very good. Is that what you want?' Lavretsky uttered with an effort. 'Certainly, I consent to that too.'

Varvara Pavlovna darted a swift glance at him, but Marya Dmitrievna cried: 'There, God be thanked!' and again drew Varvara Pavlovna forward by the arm. 'Take her now from my arms——'

'Stop a minute, I tell you,' Lavretsky interrupted her, 'I agree to live with you, Varvara Pavlovna,' he continued, 'that is to say, I will conduct you to Lavriky, and I will live there with you, as long as I can endure it, and then I will go away—and will come back again. You see, I do not want to deceive you; but do not demand anything more. You would laugh yourself if I were to carry out the desire of our respected cousin, were to press you to my breast, and to fall to assuring you that . . . that the past had not been; and the felled tree can bud again. But I see, I must submit. You will not understand these words . . . but that's no matter. I repeat, I will live with you . . . or no, I cannot promise that . . . I will be reconciled with you, I will regard you as my wife again.'

'Give her, at least, your hand on it,' observed Marya Dmitrievna, whose tears had long since dried up.

'I have never deceived Varvara Pavlovna hitherto,' returned Lavretsky; 'she will believe me without that. I will take her to Lavriky; and remember, Varvara Pavlovna, our treaty is to be reckoned as broken directly you go away from Lavriky. And now allow me to take leave.'

He bowed to both the ladies, and hurriedly went away.

'Are you not going to take her with you!' Marya Dmitrievna cried after him. . . . 'Leave him alone,' Varvara Pavlovna whispered to her. And at once she embraced her, and began thanking her, kissing her hands and calling her her saviour.

Marya Dmitrievna received her caresses indulgently; but at heart she was discontented with Lavretsky, with Varvara Pavlovna, and with the whole scene she had prepared. Very little sentimentality had come of it; Varvara Pavlovna, in her opinion, ought to have flung herself at her husband's feet.

'How was it you didn't understand me?' she commented: 'I kept saying "down".'

'It is better as it was, dear auntie; do not be uneasy—it was all for the best,' Varvara Pavlovna assured her.

'Well, any way, he's as cold as ice,' observed Marya Dmitrievna. 'You didn't weep, it is true, but I was in floods of tears before his eyes. He wants to shut you up at Lavriky. Why, won't you even be able to come and see me? All men are unfeeling,' she concluded, with a significant shake of the head.

'But then women can appreciate goodness and noble-heartedness,' said Varvara Pavlovna, and gently dropping on her knees before Marya Dmitrievna, she flung her arms about her round person, and pressed her face against it. That face wore a sly smile, but Marya Dmitrievna's tears began to flow again.

When Lavretsky returned home, he locked himself in his valet's room, and flung himself on a sofa; he lay like that till morning.

∗ 44 ∗

The following day was Sunday. The sound of bells ringing for early mass did not wake Lavretsky—he had not closed his eyes all night—but it reminded him of another Sunday, when at Lisa's desire he had gone to church. He got up hastily; some secret voice told him that he would see her there today. He went noiselessly out of the house, leaving a message for Varvara Pavlovna that he would be back to dinner, and with long strides he made his way in the direction in which the monotonously mournful bells were calling him. He arrived early; there was scarcely any one in the church; a deacon was reading the service in the choir; the measured drone of his voice—sometimes broken by a cough—fell and rose at even intervals. Lavretsky placed himself not far from the entrance. Worshippers came in one by one, stopped, crossed themselves, and bowed in all directions; their steps rang out in the empty, silent church, echoing back distinctly under the arched roof. An infirm poor little old woman in a worn-out cloak with a hood was on her knees near Lavretsky, praying assiduously; her toothless, yellow, wrinkled face expressed intense emotion; her red eyes were gazing fixedly upwards at the holy figures on the iconostasis; her bony hand was constantly coming out from under her cloak, and slowly and earnestly making a great sign of the cross. A peasant with a bushy beard and a surly face, dishevelled and unkempt, came into the church, and at once fell on both knees, and began directly crossing himself in haste, bending back his head with a shake after each prostration. Such bitter grief was expressed in his face, and in all his actions, that Lavretsky made up his mind to go up to him and ask him what was wrong. The peasant timidly and morosely started back, looked at him. . . . 'My son is dead,' he articulated quickly, and again fell to bowing to the earth. 'What could replace the consolations of the Church to them?' thought Lavretsky; and he tried himself to pray, but his heart was hard and heavy, and his thoughts were far away. He kept expecting Lisa, but Lisa did not come. The church began to be full of people; but still she was not there. The service commenced, the deacon had already read the gospel, they began ringing for the last prayer; Lavretsky moved a little forward—and suddenly caught sight of Lisa. She had come before him, but he had not seen her; she was hidden in a recess between the wall and the choir, and neither moved nor looked round. Lavretsky did not take his eyes off her till the very end of the service; he was saying farewell to her. The people began to disperse, but she still remained; it seemed as though she were waiting for Lavretsky to go out. At last she crossed herself for the last time and went out—there was only a maid with her—not turning round. Lavretsky went out of the church after her and overtook her in the street; she was walking very quickly, with downcast head, and a veil over her face.

'Good-morning, Lisaveta Mihalovna,' he said aloud with assumed carelessness: 'may I accompany you?'

She made no reply; he walked beside her.

'Are you content with me?' he asked her, dropping his voice. 'Have you heard what happened yesterday?'

'Yes, yes,' she replied in a whisper, 'that was well.' And she went still more quickly.

'Are you content?'

Lisa only bent her head in assent.

'Fedor Ivanitch,' she began in a calm but faint voice, 'I wanted to beg you not to come to see us any more; go away as soon as possible, we may see each other again later—sometime—in a year. But now, do this for my sake; fulfil my request, for God's sake.'

'I am ready to obey you in everything Lisaveta Mihalovna; but are we really to part like this? will you not say one word to me?'

'Fedor Ivanitch, you are walking near me now. . . . But already you are so far from me. And not only you, but——'

'Speak out, I entreat you!' cried Lavretsky, 'what do you mean?'

'You will hear, perhaps . . . but whatever it may be, forget . . . no, do not forget; remember me.'

'Me forget you——'

'That's enough, good-bye. Do not come after me.'

'Lisa!' Lavretsky was beginning.

'Good-bye, good-bye!' she repeated, pulling her veil still lower and almost running forward. Lavretsky looked after her, and with bowed head, turned back along the street. He stumbled up against Lemm, who was also walking along with his eyes on the ground, and his hat pulled down to his nose.

They looked at one another without speaking.

'Well, what have you to say?' Lavretsky brought out at last.

'What have I to say?' returned Lemm, grimly. 'I have nothing to say. All is dead, and we are dead (*Alles ist tot, und wir sind tot*). So you're going to the right, are you?'

'Yes.'

'And I to the left. Good-bye.'

The following morning Fedor Ivanitch set off with his wife for Lavriky. She drove in front in the carriage with Ada and Justine; he behind, in the coach. The pretty little girl did not move away from the window the whole journey; she was astonished at everything: the peasants, the women, the wells, the yokes over the horses' heads, the bells and the flocks of crows. Justine shared her wonder. Varvara Pavlovna laughed at their remarks and exclamations. She was in excellent spirits; before leaving the town, she had come to an explanation with her husband.

'I understand your position,' she said to him, and from the look in her subtle eyes, he was able to infer that she understood his position fully, 'but you must do me, at least, this justice, that I am easy to live with; I will not fetter you or hinder you; I wanted to secure Ada's future, I want nothing more.'

'Well, you have obtained your object,' observed Fedor Ivanitch.

'I only dream of one thing now: to hide myself for ever in obscurity. I shall remember your goodness always.'

'Enough of that,' he interrupted.

'And I shall know how to respect your independence and tranquillity,' she went on, completing the phrases she had prepared.

Lavretsky made her a low bow. Varvara Pavlovna then believed her husband was thanking her in his heart.

On the evening of the next day they reached Lavriky; a week later, Lavretsky set off for Moscow, leaving his wife five thousand roubles for her household expenses; and the day after Lavretsky's departure, Panshin made his appearance. Varvara Pavlovna had begged him not to forget her in her solitude. She gave him the best possible reception, and, till a late hour of the night, the lofty apartments of the house and even the garden re-echoed with the sound of music, singing, and lively French talk. For three days Varvara Pavlovna entertained Panshin; when he took leave of her, warmly pressing her lovely hands, he promised to come back very soon—and he kept his word.

Lisa had a room to herself on the second storey of her
mother's house, a clean bright little room with a little white
bed, with pots of flowers in the corners and before the
windows, a small writing-table, a book-stand, and a crucifix
on the wall. It was always called the nursery; Lisa had been
born in it. When she returned from the church where she
had seen Lavretsky she set everything in her room in order
more carefully than usual, dusted it everywhere, looked
through and tied up with ribbon all her copybooks, and the
letters of her girl-friends, shut up all the drawers, watered
the flowers and caressed every blossom with her hand. All
this she did without haste, noiselessly, with a kind of rapt
and gentle solicitude on her face. She stopped at last in the
middle of the room, slowly looked round, and going up to the
table above which the crucifix was hanging, she fell on her
knees, dropped her head on to her clasped hands and remained motionless.

Marfa Timofyevna came in and found her in this position.
Lisa did not observe her entrance. The old lady stepped out
on tip-toe and coughed loudly several times outside the door.
Lisa rose quickly and wiped her eyes, which were bright with
unshed tears.

'Ah! I see, you have been setting your cell to rights
again,' observed Marfa Timofyevna, and she bent low over a
young rose-tree in a pot; 'how nice it smells!'

Lisa looked thoughtfully at her aunt.

'How strange you should use that word!' she murmured.

'What word, eh?' the old lady returned quickly. 'What do
you mean? This is horrible,' she began, suddenly flinging off
her cap and sitting down on Lisa's little bed: 'it is more than
I can bear! this is the fourth day now that I have been boiling
over inside; I can't pretend not to notice any longer; I can't
see you getting pale, and fading away, and weeping, I can't,
I can't!'

'Why, what is the matter, auntie?' said Lisa, 'it's nothing.'

'Nothing!' cried Marfa Timofyevna; 'you may tell that to
others but not to me. Nothing, who was on her knees just

this minute? and whose eyelashes are still wet with tears? Nothing, indeed! why, look at yourself, what have you done with your face, what has become of your eyes?—Nothing! do you suppose I don't know all?'

'It will pass off, auntie; give me time.'

'It will pass off, but when? Good God! Merciful Saviour! can you have loved him like this? why, he's an old man, Lisa, darling. There, I don't dispute he's a good fellow, no harm in him; but what of that? we are all good people, the world is not so small, there will be always plenty of that commodity.'

'I tell you, it will all pass away, it has all passed away already.'

'Listen, Lisa, darling, what I am going to say to you,' Marfa Timofyevna said suddenly, making Lisa sit beside her, and straightening her hair and her neckerchief. 'It seems to you now in the midst of the worst of it that nothing can ever heal your sorrow. Ah, my darling, the only thing that can't be cured is death. You only say to yourself now: "I won't give in to it—so there!" and you will be surprised yourself how soon, how easily it will pass off. Only have patience.'

'Auntie,' returned Lisa, 'it has passed off already, it is all over.'

'Passed! how has it passed? Why, your poor little nose has grown sharp already and you say it is over. A fine way of getting over it!'

'Yes, it is over, auntie, if you will only try to help me,' Lisa declared with sudden animation, and she flung herself on Marfa Timofyevna's neck. 'Dear auntie, be a friend to me, help me, don't be angry, understand me' . . .

'Why, what is it, what is it, my good girl? Don't terrify me, please; I shall scream directly; don't look at me like that; tell me quickly what is it?'

'I—I want,' Lisa hid her face on Marfa Timofyevna's bosom, 'I want to go into a convent,' she articulated faintly.

The old lady almost bounded off the bed.

'Cross yourself, my girl, Lisa, dear, think what you are saying; what are you thinking of? God have mercy on you!' she stammered at last. 'Lie down, my darling, sleep a little, all this comes from sleeplessness, my dearie.'

Lisa raised her head, her cheeks were glowing.

'No, auntie,' she said, 'don't speak like that; I have made up my mind, I prayed, I asked counsel of God; all is at an end, my life with you is at an end. Such a lesson was not for nothing; and it is not the first time that I have thought of it. Happiness was not for me; even when I had hopes of happiness, my heart was always heavy. I knew all my own sins and those of others, and how papa made our fortune; I know it all. For all that there must be expiation. I am sorry for you, sorry for mamma, for Lenotchka; but there is no help; I feel that there is no living here for me; I have taken leave of all, I have greeted everything in the house for the last time; something calls to me; I am sick at heart, I want to hide myself away for ever. Do not hinder me, do not dissuade me, help me, or else I must go away alone.'

Marfa Timofyevna listened to her niece with horror.

'She is ill, she is raving,' she thought: 'we must send for a doctor; but for which one? Gedeonovsky was praising one the other day; he always tells lies—but perhaps this time he spoke the truth.' But when she was convinced that Lisa was not ill, and was not raving, when she constantly made the same answer to all her expostulations, Marfa Timofyevna was alarmed and distressed in earnest. 'But you don't know, my darling,' she began to reason with her, 'what a life it is in those convents! Why, they would feed you, my own, on green hemp oil, and they would put you in the coarsest, coarsest linen, and make you go about in the cold; you will never be able to bear all that, Lisa, darling. All this is Agafya's doing; she led you astray. But then you know she began by living and lived for her own pleasure; you must live too. At least, let me die in peace, and then do as you like. And who has ever heard of such a thing, for the sake of such a—for the sake of a goat's beard, God forgive us!—for the sake of a man—to go into a convent! Why, if you are so sick at heart, go on a pilgrimage, offer prayers to some saint, have a *Te Deum* sung, but don't put the black hood on your head, my dear creature, my good girl.'

And Marfa Timofyevna wept bitterly.

Lisa comforted her, wiped away her tears and wept herself, but remained unshaken. In her despair Marfa Timofyevna had recourse to threats: to tell her mother all about it . . . but that too was of no avail. Only at the old lady's most earnest entreaties Lisa agreed to put off carrying out her plan for six months. Marfa Timofyevna was obliged to promise in return that if, within six months, she did not change her mind, she would herself help her and would do all she could to gain Marya Dmitrievna's consent.

In spite of her promise to bury herself in seclusion, at the first approach of cold weather, Varvara Pavlovna, having provided herself with funds, removed to Petersburg, where she took a modest but charming set of apartments, found for her by Panshin, who had left the O—— district a little before. During the later part of his residence in O—— he had completely lost Marya Dmitrievna's good graces; he had suddenly given up visiting her and scarcely stirred from Lavriky. Varvara Pavlovna had enslaved him, literally enslaved him, no other word can describe her boundless, irresistible, unquestioned sway over him.

Lavretsky spent the winter in Moscow; and in the spring of the following year the news reached him that Lisa had taken the veil in the B—— convent, in one of the remote parts of Russia.

EPILOGUE

Eight years had passed by. Once more the spring had come. . . . But we will say a few words first of the fate of Mihalevitch, Panshin, and Madame Lavretsky—and then take leave of them. Mihalevitch, after long wanderings, has at last fallen in with exactly the right work for him; he has received the position of senior superintendent of a government school. He is very well content with his lot; his pupils adore him, though they mimic him too. Panshin has gained great advancement in rank, and already has a directorship in view; he walks with a slight stoop, caused doubtless by the weight round his neck of the Vladimir cross which has been conferred on him. The official in him has finally gained the ascendency over the artist; his still youngish face has grown yellow, and his hair scanty; he now neither sings nor sketches, but applies himself in secret to literature; he has written a comedy, in the style of a 'proverb', and as nowadays all writers have to draw a portrait of someone or something, he has drawn in it the portrait of a coquette, and he reads it privately to two or three ladies who look kindly upon him. He has, however, not entered upon matrimony, though many excellent opportunities of doing so have presented themselves. For this Varvara Pavlovna was responsible. As for her, she lives constantly at Paris, as in former days. Fedor Ivanitch has given her a promissory note for a large sum, and has so secured immunity from the possibility of her making a second sudden descent upon him. She has grown older and stouter. but is still charming and elegant. Everyone has his ideal, Varvara Pavlovna found hers in the dramatic works of M. Dumas Fils. She diligently frequents the theatres, when consumptive and sentimental 'dames aux camélias' are brought on the stage; to be Madame Doche seems to her the height of human bliss; she once declared that she did not desire a better fate for her own daughter. It is to be hoped that fate will spare Mademoiselle Ada from such happiness; from a rosy-cheeked, chubby child she has turned into a weak-chested, pale girl; her nerves are already deranged. The number of Varvara Pavlovna's adorers has diminished, but she still has some; a few she will probably retain to the end of her days. The most ardent of them in these later days is a certain Zakurdalo-Skubirnikov, a retired guardsman, a full-bearded man of thirty-eight, of exceptionally vigorous physique. The French *habitués* of Madame Lavretsky's salon call him '*le gros taureau de l' Ukrāine*'; Varvara Pavlovna never invites him to her fashionable evening reunions, but he is in the fullest enjoyment of her favours.

And so—eight years have passed by. Once more the breezes of spring breathed brightness and rejoicing from the heavens; once more spring was smiling upon the earth and upon men; once more under her caresses everything was turning to blossom, to love, to song. The town of O—— had undergone little change in the course of these eight years; but Marya Dmitrievna's house seemed to have grown younger; its freshly-painted walls gave a bright welcome, and the panes of its open windows were crimson, shining in the setting sun; from these windows the light merry sound of ringing young voices and continual laughter floated into the street; the whole house seemed astir with life and brimming over with gaiety. The lady of the house herself had long been in her tomb; Marya Dmitrievna had died two years after Lisa took the veil, and Marfa Timofyevna had not long survived her niece; they lay side by side in the cemetery of the town. Nastasya Karpovna too was no more; for several years the faithful old woman had gone every week to say a prayer over her friend's ashes. . . . Her time had come, and now her bones too lay in the damp earth. But Marya Dmitrievna's house had not passed into strangers' hands, it had not gone out of her family, the home had not been broken up. Lenotchka, transformed into a slim, beautiful young girl, and her betrothed lover—a fair-haired officer of hussars; Marya Dmitrievna's son, who had just been married in Petersburg and had come with his young wife for the spring to O——; his wife's sister, a school-girl of sixteen, with glowing cheeks and bright eyes; Shurotchka, grown up and also pretty, made up the youthful household, whose laughter and talk set the walls of the Kalitins' house resounding. Everything in the house was changed, everything was in keeping with its new inhabitants. Beardless servant lads, grinning and full of fun, had replaced the sober old servants of former days. Two setter dogs dashed wildly about and gambolled over the sofas, where the fat Roska had at one time waddled in solemn dignity. The stables were filled with slender racers, spirited carriage horses, fiery out-riders with plaited manes, and riding horses from the Don. The breakfast, dinner, and supper-hours were all in confusion and disorder; in the words of the neighbours, 'unheard-of arrangements' were made.

On the evening of which we are speaking, the inhabitants of the Kalitins' house (the eldest of them, Lenotchka's betrothed, was only twenty-four) were engaged in a game, which, though not of a very complicated nature, was, to judge from their merry laughter, exceedingly entertaining to them; they were running about the rooms, chasing one another; the dogs, too, were running and barking, and the canaries, hanging in cages above the windows, were straining their throats in rivalry and adding to the general uproar by the shrill trilling of their piercing notes. At the very height of this deafening merrymaking a mud-bespattered carriage stopped at the gate, and a man of five-and-forty, in a travelling dress, stepped out of it and stood still in amazement. He stood a little time without stirring, watching the house with attentive eyes; then went through the little gate in the court-yard, and slowly mounted the steps. In the hall he met no one; but the door of a room was suddenly flung open, and out of it rushed Shurotchka, flushed and hot, and instantly, with a ringing shout, all the young party in pursuit of her. They stopped short at once and were quiet at the sight of a stranger; but their clear eyes fixed on him wore the same friendly expression, and their fresh faces were still smiling as Marya Dmitrievna's son went up to the visitor and asked him cordially what he could do for him.

'I am Lavretsky,' replied the visitor.

He was answered by a shout in chorus—and not because these young people were greatly delighted at the arrival of a distant, almost forgotten relation, but simply because they were ready to be delighted and make a noise at every opportunity. They surrounded Lavretsky at once; Lenotchka, as an old acquaintance, was the first to mention her own name, and assured him that in a little while she would have certainly recognised him. She presented him to the rest of the party, calling each, even her betrothed, by their pet names. They all trooped through the dining-room into the drawing-room. The walls of both rooms had been re-papered; but the furniture remained the same. Lavretsky recognised the piano; even the embroidery-frame in the window was just the same, and in the same position, and it seemed with the same unfinished embroidery on it, as eight years ago. They made him sit down in a comfortable arm-chair; all sat down politely in a circle round him. Questions, exclamations, and anecdotes followed.

'It's a long time since we have seen you,' observed Lenotchka simply, 'and Varvara Pavlovna we have seen nothing of either.'

'Well, no wonder!' her brother hastened to interpose. 'I carried you off to Petersburg, and Fedor Ivanitch has been living all the time in the country.'

'Yes, and mamma died soon after then.'

'And Marfa Timofyevna,' observed Shurotchka.

'And Nastasya Karpovna,' added Lenotchka, 'and Monsieur Lemm.'

'What? is Lemm dead?' inquired Lavretsky.

'Yes,' replied young Kalitin, 'he left here for Odessa; they say someone enticed him there; and there he died.'

'You don't happen to know, . . . did he leave any music?'

'I don't know; not very likely.'

All were silent and looked about them. A slight cloud of melancholy flitted over all the young faces.

'But Matross is alive,' said Lenotchka suddenly.

'And Gedeonovsky,' added her brother.

At Gedeonovsky's name a merry laugh broke out at once.

'Yes, he is alive, and as great a liar as ever,' Marya Dmitrievna's son continued; 'and only fancy, yesterday this madcap'—pointing to the school-girl, his wife's sister—'put some pepper in his snuff-box.'

'How he did sneeze!' cried Lenotchka, and again there was a burst of unrestrained laughter.

'We have had news of Lisa lately,' observed young Kalitin,

and again a hush fell upon all; 'there was good news of her; she is recovering her health a little now.'

'She is still in the same convent?' Lavretsky asked, not without some effort.

'Yes, still in the same.'

'Does she write to you?'

'No, never; but we get news through other people.'

A sudden and profound silence followed. 'A good angel is passing over,' all were thinking.

'Wouldn't you like to go into the garden?' said Kalitin, turning to Lavretsky; 'it is very nice now, though we have let it run wild a little.'

Lavretsky went out into the garden, and the first thing that met his eyes was the very garden seat on which he had once spent with Lisa those few blissful moments, never repeated; it had grown black and warped; but he recognised it, and his soul was filled with that emotion, unequalled for sweetness and for bitterness—the emotion of keen sorrow for vanished youth, for the happiness which has once been possessed. He walked along the avenues with the young people; the lime-trees looked hardly older or taller in the eight years, but their shade was thicker; on the other hand, all the bushes had sprung up, the raspberry bushes had grown strong, the hazels were a tangled thicket, and from all sides rose the fresh scent of the trees and grass and lilac.

'This would be a nice place for Puss-in-the-Corner,' cried Lenotchka suddenly, as they came upon a small green lawn, surrounded by lime-trees, 'and we are just five, too.'

'Have you forgotten Fedor Ivanitch?' replied her brother, . . . 'or didn't you count yourself?'

Lenotchka blushed slightly.

'But would Fedor Ivanitch, at his age——' she began.

'Please, play your games,' Lavretsky hastened to interpose; 'don't pay attention to me. I shall be happier myself, when I am sure I am not in your way. And there's no need for you to entertain me; we old fellows have an occupation which you know nothing of yet, and which no amusement can replace— our memories.'

The young people listened to Lavretsky with polite, but rather ironical respect—as though a teacher were giving

[163]

them a lesson—and suddenly they all dispersed, and ran to the lawn; four stood near trees, one in the middle, and the game began.

And Lavretsky went back into the house, went into the dining-room, drew near the piano and touched one of the keys; it gave out a faint but clear sound; on that note had begun the inspired melody with which long ago on that same happy night Lemm, the dead Lemm, had thrown him into such transports. Then Lavretsky went into the drawing-room, and for a long time he did not leave it; in that room where he had so often seen Lisa, her image rose most vividly before him; he seemed to feel the traces of her presence round him; but his grief for her was crushing, not easy to bear; it had none of the peace which comes with death. Lisa still lived somewhere, hidden and afar; he thought of her as of the living, but he did not recognise the girl he had once loved in that dim pale shadow, cloaked in a nun's dress and encircled in misty clouds of incense. Lavretsky would not have recognised himself, could he have looked at himself, as mentally he looked at Lisa. In the course of these eight years he had passed that turning-point in life, which many never pass, but without which no one can be a good man to the end; he had really ceased to think of his own happiness, of his personal aims. He had grown calm, and—why hide the truth?—he had grown old not only in face and in body, he had grown old in heart; to keep a young heart up to old age, as some say, is not only difficult, but almost ridiculous; he may well be content who has not lost his belief in goodness, his steadfast will, and his zeal for work. Lavretsky had good reason to be content; he had become actually an excellent farmer, he had really learnt to cultivate the land, and his labours were not only for himself; he had, to the best of his powers, secured on a firm basis the welfare of his peasants.

Lavretsky went out of the house into the garden, and sat down on the familiar garden seat. And on this loved spot, facing the house where for the last time he had vainly stretched out his hand for the enchanted cup which frothed and sparkled with the golden wine of delight, he, a solitary homeless wanderer, looked back upon his life, while the joyous shouts of the younger generation who were already filling his place floated across the garden to him. His heart was sad, but not weighed down, nor bitter; much there was to regret, nothing to be ashamed of.

'Play away, be gay, grow strong, vigorous youth!' he thought, and there was no bitterness in his meditations; 'your life is before you, and for you life will be easier; you have not, as we had, to find out a path for yourselves, to struggle, to fall, and to rise again in the dark; we had enough to do to last out—and how many of us did not last out?—but you need only do your duty, work away, and the blessing of an old man be with you. For me, after today, after these emotions, there remains to take my leave at last—and though sadly, without envy, without any dark feelings, to say, in sight of the end, in sight of God who awaits me: "Welcome, lonely old age! burn out, useless life!" '

Lavretsky quietly rose and quietly went away; no one noticed him, no one detained him; the joyous cries sounded more loudly in the garden behind the thick green wall of high lime-trees. He took his seat in the carriage and bade the coachman drive home and not hurry the horses.

'And the end?' perhaps the dissatisfied reader will inquire. 'What became of Lavretsky afterwards, and of Lisa?' But what is there to tell of people who, though still alive, have withdrawn from the battlefield of life? They say, Lavretsky visited that remote convent where Lisa had hidden herself— that he saw her. Crossing over from choir to choir, she walked close past him, moving with the even, hurried, but meek walk of a nun; and she did not glance at him; only the eyelashes on the side towards him quivered a little, only she bent her emaciated face lower, and the fingers of her clasped hands, entwined with her rosary, were pressed still closer to one another. What were they both thinking, what were they feeling? Who can know? who can say? There are such moments in life, there are such feelings . . . One can but point to them—and pass them by.

THE END